Unraveling a Dangerous Case . . .

"So what's the case?" Frank asked the screen impatiently.

"The case has to do with the legendary Tomb of the Golden Mummy. Perhaps you've heard the story? It says that somewhere in the heart of the desert, beyond the Valley of the Serpents, lies the richest tomb in all of Egypt, a maze built into the side of a cliff.

"It is the tomb of Pharaoh Semerkhet III—known as the Golden Mummy, because he was supposedly buried with more golden implements and statues than any other pharaoh before or since."

Q kept talking as the screen showed scenes of archaeological digs near the pyramids. *"Until last year, everyone assumed that the Golden Mummy and its tomb were just legend. Then, last year, rumors started going around that Roger Corson had found the tomb."*

I hit the pause button. "Roger Corson? He's that explorer guy who dates all the supermodels, right?"

"Yeah, that's him. He's always in the news."

"Hey, Frank, didn't Corson—"

"Good memory, Joe," Frank said. "The papers said he died 'under mysterious circumstances.'"

"Whoa." I sat down on the edge of my bed and hit play.

THE HARDY BOYS

UNDERCOVER BROTHERS™

Available from Simon & Schuster

THE HARDY BOYS

UNDERCOVER BROTHERS™

#13 The Mummy's Curse

FRANKLIN W. DIXON

ALADDIN PAPERBACKS
An imprint of Simon & Schuster
Children's Publishing Division
1230 Avenue of the Americas
New York, NY 10020

Designed by Lisa Vega
The text of this book was set in Aldine 401 BT.
Manufactured in the United States of America
First Aladdin Paperbacks edition February 2006
2 4 6 8 10 9 7 5 3 1

Library of Congress Control Number: 2005920540
ISBN-13: 978-1-4169-1507-2
ISBN-10: 1-4169-1507-4

Aladdin Paperbacks
New York   London   Toronto   Sydney

This book is a work of fiction. Any references to historical events, real people, or real locales are used fictitiously. Other names, characters, places, and incidents are the product of the author's imagination, and any resemblance to actual events or locales or persons, living or dead, is entirely coincidental.

❤ALADDIN PAPERBACKS
An imprint of Simon & Schuster
Children's Publishing Division
1230 Avenue of the Americas,
New York, NY 10020

Copyright © 2006 by Simon & Schuster, Inc.
All rights reserved, including the right of
reproduction in whole or in part in any form.
THE HARDY BOYS MYSTERY STORIES and HARDY BOYS UNDER-
COVER BROTHERS are trademarks of Simon & Schuster, Inc.
ALADDIN PAPERBACKS and colophon are trademarks of
Simon & Schuster, Inc.
Designed by Lisa Vega
The text of this book was set in font Aldine 401BT.
Manufactured in the United States of America
First Aladdin Paperbacks edition November 2006
20 19 18 17 16 15 14 13 12 11

Library of Congress Control Number 2006922950
ISBN-13: 978-1-4169-1507-2
0118 QVE

TABLE OF CONTENTS

FRANK

1.

Down a Dark Alley

Usually, when Joe and I race, it's to see who's faster.
This time? We were running for our lives.

I'm not just saying that. The five nasty characters chasing us through the back alleys of Cairo, Egypt, were very, very real. We're talking long, curved knives in their teeth, sharp machetes in their hands, and a look of sheer murder in their eyes.

If they ever caught up with us, killing us would be just the *start* of it.

I have to say, they were pretty fast on their feet. I mean, Joe and I run track for Bayport High, and we have a ton of medals to show for it. It's amazing these guys were even keeping up, what with all the hardware they were carrying. But they were gaining on us.

To be fair to me and Joe, we didn't know these streets—we had come to Egypt strictly as tourists. It was only a chance encounter on our first night here—namely, a body falling from the roof, right past our hotel window—that had landed us right in the middle of an international drug cartel turf war.

Nice, eh?

We didn't know our way around these Old Cairo neighborhoods with their narrow, winding streets, and there was no time to consult a map now. I felt like a mouse in a maze, and Joe looked totally clueless.

The drug smugglers chasing us weren't from around here either. From their whispers, we figured they were French, Russian, and Burmese—but they seemed to know the neighborhood a whole lot better than we did. No wonder, really. We'd done a little digging and learned they'd been doing business in Cairo for at least a year when we stumbled on their operation and blew it wide open.

It was after midnight, but the streets of the Egyptian capital were crammed full of people. This city is home to about twenty million, so I guess we shouldn't have been surprised that a few million were still out and about.

Still, it made it hard to get away. We kept bumping

into stuff that slowed us down—market carts, bicycles left on the sidewalk, and lots of slow-moving Cairenes (that's what they call themselves).

None of that slowed the crooks down, though—when you have knives and machetes on you, people tend to get out of your way.

By the time we ran into our fourth (or was it the fifth?) blind alley, it was too late to get back out. Our five foul "friends" blocked the entrance, brandishing their blades at us.

Yikes.

"Okay, Joe, how are your kung fu moves? You still in practice?"

"Uh . . . kind of. It's been a while."

"Well, just think of that movie we saw last week. Be like that guy."

"Jackie Chan? Sure thing—that's me," he said, giving me a wink. Nothing scares Joe. Me, I'm allergic to sharp knives—the kind we were facing now. The bad guys came at us all at once—not like in the movies, where they're polite and come at you one at a time.

Luckily, the narrowness of the alley played to our advantage. It squeezed them into a tightly packed ball.

At the last possible instant, Joe and I sprang into action. We dove into twin low rolls, bowling three of our assailants over. Two were so surprised they dropped their machetes—and Joe and I grabbed them.

"Now I feel better," I said. No matter how hard you karate chop a sharp knife, you're going to get the worst of it. Now that we were armed, I liked our chances a whole lot more. We swung our machetes in a blur of motion, keeping the five men at bay.

They couldn't come at us down the alley without running straight into the blades and being cut to pieces, so they hung back, looking at each other for inspiration. None of them was willing to go first—and we were blocking the front of the alley. There was no escape except through us, and our flying machetes.

Of course, this was just temporary. We couldn't keep it up for very long. My arms were already feeling exhausted.

One of the attackers put his machete back in its sheath and grabbed a garbage can instead. He threw the lid to one of his buddies to use as a shield, and then grabbed the handles of the can, holding it in front of him like a battering ram.

Uh-oh.

They slowly advanced on us. We backed up toward the street.

I glanced over at Joe, and he nodded back. We'd been in situations like this together many times, and we each knew exactly what the other was thinking.

We could try to hold them here in this alley until the police arrived. . . .

Or we could make another run for it. If we ran, though, they would catch up to us sooner or later.

I heard sirens in the distance. "Boy, I sure hope they're coming for us."

We were wearing GPS tracking devices, so, assuming they were working, Captain Ali and his men should have been on our trail the whole time. We'd planned this in advance. On the other hand, in this city of mazes and blind alleys, they could easily have gotten as lost as we had.

No, the sirens were definitely getting closer. The only trouble was, we were running out of blind alley to back up into. Soon we'd be out in the street, where they could easily surround us. We had them trapped for the moment, but the police would never make it in time to turn the tide.

We needed to go to Plan B.

Whatever that was.

Now, I'm the idea guy in moments like this. That's not to say Joe doesn't come up with a brilliant plan every once in a while—but I knew we

5

were both counting on me to get us out of this one.

"You remember the last blind alley we ran into, before this one?" I asked him.

"Yeah, I guess."

"Could you find it again if we made a run for it and got separated?"

"No way."

"Okay, just follow me then."

"What? You want to run, and then get trapped in another dead end? I like it better this way, with us on the outside, so we can escape if we have to."

"Joe, we need to set up the gizmo."

"Huh?"

"The *gizmo*—the free sample from the convention, remember?"

"Which one?"

I looked at the advancing assassins. They were so close now we had to keep moving back toward the street. My arm was falling off from all the machete-waving, and I was sure Joe's was too.

I couldn't describe which gizmo, or I'd give it away. One of these clowns was sure to speak English.

Then it hit me—Pig Latin!

"Ee-they ip-tray ire-way!"

"Huh?"

"Figure it out, okay? One, two—go!"

We turned and ran out of that alley before the five dirtbags knew what hit them. They dropped the garbage can and lid and started after us, stumbling over each other and giving us a good head start.

I led Joe back down the streets we'd just traveled— only this time I knew what to expect and where I was heading. That really helped—we gained some distance from our pursuers, who seemed not to have realized where we were heading.

I needed about ten seconds to make this work— ten seconds between the time we got to the alley and the time *they* got there.

Ten seconds to set the trip wire.

Ah, yes, Plan B—when your fighting skills will only get you so far, go high-tech!

I'll back up a little.

We had come to Egypt with our dad, Fenton Hardy. He'd been invited to give the keynote speech at the International Security Forces Convention, which was being held at one of the fanciest hotels in the world, the Cairo Inter-Continental.

And since none of us had ever been to Egypt, Dad decided to bring the whole family along—me, Joe, Mom, and Aunt Trudy.

While Dad was busy with the convention, Mom

and Trudy had spent most of the week touring Cairo's famous museums and seeing the pyramids and the Sphinx.

Joe and I would have gone with them, but we got distracted by that body falling past our window. (We're like our dad—we never can turn away when a crime's been committed.)

One of the great things about conventions is the free gizmos you get. This being a security convention, there were all kinds of giveaways—everything from flexible handcuffs to stun grenades (Joe took one, and I sure hoped he still had it in his pocket!) to trip wires.

Now we were about to find out if our free samples really worked.

The trip wire is a neat little gadget. It's as old as the hills, really—the pygmies have used them to trap game for thousands of years. It's like a tape measure reel. You pull it out, string it, and then it snaps back when you're done.

Joe and I spread ours across the alley, about ankle-high, and attached both ends with the superstick Velcro pads that came with it.

"Now what?" Joe asked. "Do we hide?"

"No—we stand right here," I said.

"Oh, I get it—we're the bait!"

The thugs reached the entrance to the alley,

caught a glimpse of us standing there, and made a quick beeline for us. When the first one hit the trip wire, they all went down like bowling pins, one on top of the other.

Joe and I leaped at them, grabbing more of their weapons before they could recover. I conked one on the head with a machete handle, aiming right for the sweet spot at the back of the neck. Then I cuffed him with a pair of flexible cuffs.

One down, four more to go.

Joe was cuffing a guy on the other side of the pile. "Got that stun grenade?" I asked him, as the other three bad guys got to their feet and retrieved their weapons.

"Aw, man, I was gonna save that!"

"Use it now, brother!"

He didn't argue. Pulling the pin, he tossed it right at the feet of the three remaining bad guys, who were just raising their weapons to deliver the fatal blows to me and Joe.

ZZZAPP.

No bang, no loud noise—just the sound of nerve cells frying, and the thud of three hulking hoodlums hitting the pavement like three tons of bricks.

We had them cuffed in a matter of seconds and were collecting their weapons when Captain Ali's

9

police car screeched to a halt in front of the alley. Four more cars, sirens blaring and lights flashing, pulled up right behind it.

"Well, well, what have we here?" Ali asked as he came toward us. He wore a big smile under his thick black mustache, and his eyes were gleaming. "It seems as if we've arrived too late to see the show!"

"How'd it go on your end?" I asked him.

"We found the gang's leaders right where you told us they would be," he said, with a little bow and a tip of his police cap. "I must say, you boys are not bad at this—not bad at all, for a pair of amateurs."

Amateurs?

If he only knew!

2.

How Bazaar, How Bizarre

"Come inside here, gentlemen. What would you like? I sell many fine items."

"This way, this way! My prices are cheaper! I promise you, you'll buy my wares if you see them!"

"*As Salaam Alaikum!* Good morning! Welcome to my shop! Please, come inside!"

All these invitations and more were coming at me and Frank as we walked down the main street of Cairo's biggest, oldest bazaar. They were coming in English, too—most Egyptians who deal with tourists and other foreigners speak English (the Brits governed this place for a long time back in the day).

"No thanks—just looking," we kept saying, but none of the merchants seemed to believe us. One

11

or two actually pulled at our arms, trying to draw us inside their tiny shops, which were filled with lots of really cool stuff.

We weren't really shopping, though, so much as just being tourists, here in the capital of one of the greatest, oldest civilizations on Earth. The cool stuff would wait.

We'd already been in Egypt for six days. Tomorrow we were scheduled to leave for the States. Back to Bayport, and school, and friends, and our ordinary, everyday lives.

After a week of chasing and being chased by international criminals, we both felt like we'd missed the best of Egypt, like the mummies in the Cairo Museum and the treasures of King Tut. Who knew when we'd ever get the chance to see them again? To make ourselves feel better, we were trying to pack in as much as we could on our last day.

Just for fun, we let ourselves be dragged into two or three shops, where we bought a few unusual doodads to give our friends back at home: Chet, Iola, Belinda. . . .

With our plastic bags full of trinkets, we headed back through the bazaar toward the hotel. That afternoon we'd go to the Cairo Museum and finally see the mummies—one last memory of our time here to take home with us.

"Please, come inside! I have all the latest videos and CDs!"

"No, thanks," I said. "We can get CDs back home."

"Oh, no—not *these*," the merchant said. "Please, come in, and I will show you."

He was short and fat, had thick, tinted glasses, and wore a red Turkish cap on his head—a fez, I think they call it.

I pointed to the cap. "I'll buy one of those if you've got any."

Not realizing I was joking, he said, "No, this is *my* hat. I do not sell hats. Only CDs and DVDs. Please, come."

"Look," Frank broke in. "We're tired, it's almost lunchtime, and we have to get back to our hotel. Maybe some other time."

"Wait!" the man called after us as we tried to leave. "At least look at one DVD! Here—*this* one!" He pulled one from the pocket of his long white robe and held it out to us.

The DVD, a video game, was entitled "Adventure in the Desert." It had a picture of two guys on camelback riding through the desert. Chasing

13

them were five men on horseback, holding swords high in the air.

"Hey," I said, "that reminds me of last night—two of us, five of them."

"You know what else?" Frank said, staring hard at the drawing. "Those two guys on the camels look familiar."

"Huh?" I stared at them closely. One had blond hair, one dark. "Hey, wait a minute. . . ."

"Ah!" the shopkeeper said, his eyes lighting up behind the thick glasses. "You see? I told you!"

"Frank," I said, "those two guys—they're *us.*"

"A bright boy. A very smart boy," said the shopkeeper, nodding his head. "You will enjoy this game very much, I am sure."

"How much?" Frank asked.

"Special price," said the man in the fez. "For you? Free." He shoved the game into my hand.

"Thanks!" Frank said. "Come on, Joe. We've got business."

This was no ordinary video game. It was our next case!

Back in our hotel room, I took out our video game system and slipped the DVD in. The game began to load.

ADVENTURE IN THE DESERT! A NEW
ATAC ADVENTURE STARRING FRANK AND
JOE HARDY!

Nice title.

Q.T.'s round, smiling face filled the screen.
He's our boss at ATAC—American Teens Against
Crime, the secret crime-fighting organization our
dad founded and we work for as secret agents.

"Hello, boys," he said. *"Or should I say, as they do
over there,* As Salaam Alaikum—*peace be with you?"*

"Wa Alaikum Salaam," Frank and I said together
in response. *And with you also.*

*"Sorry to bother you while you're on vacation, but it so
happens we need a pair of agents over there, and since
you're already in Cairo, we thought we'd save ourselves
the airfare and put you on the case.*

*"We'll need you to stay over there for another week. I've
already cleared it with your father, although you'll have to
figure out how to break the news to the rest of your family."*

That was always the deal with ATAC; we
couldn't let anyone but our father in on our cases.
Our work was top secret.

"So what's the case?" Frank asked the screen
impatiently.

*"The case has to do with the legendary Tomb of the
Golden Mummy. Perhaps you've heard the story? It says*

that somewhere in the heart of the desert, beyond the Valley of the Serpents, lies the richest tomb in all of Egypt, a maze built into the side of a cliff.

"It is the tomb of Pharaoh Semerkhet III—known as the Golden Mummy, because he was supposedly buried with more golden implements and statues than any other pharaoh before or since."

"Wow," I said. "That would be cool, to see something like that."

"Forget it," Frank said. "Didn't you hear him say it was legendary?"

Q kept talking as the screen showed scenes of archaeological digs near the pyramids. *"Until last year, everyone assumed that the Golden Mummy and its tomb were just legend. Then rumors started going around that Roger Corson had found the tomb."*

I hit the pause button. "Roger Corson? He's that explorer guy who dates all the supermodels, right?"

"Yeah, that's him. He's always in the news."

"Hey, Frank, didn't Corson—"

"Good memory, Joe," Frank said. "The papers said he died 'under mysterious circumstances.'"

"Whoa." I sat down on the edge of my bed and hit play.

Q resumed his narration. *"Corson never admitted it*

16

publicly, but the story got out that he'd made a map of his discovery and was going to return and find the treasure. As far as anyone knew, it was only a rumor. But somebody must have believed it—because last month Corson was found murdered in his bed in his London apartment, with a four-thousand-year-old dagger stuck right through his heart."

"Sheesh!" I said.

"That really bites," Frank agreed.

"The apartment was ransacked. And a woman on that floor of the building says she saw a blood-soaked mummy fleeing the scene. Oh, by the way, according to the legend, the Golden Mummy, in addition to its priceless treasures, also comes with a curse."

"Whoa!"

"Cool," I said.

"The police reached a dead end and shelved the case," Q went on. *"And that might have been the end of it too—if it hadn't been for Samantha Chilton. I trust you've heard of her."*

"Samantha Chilton?" I repeated. "Is he kidding? Who hasn't?"

In case you just dropped in from Mars, Samantha Chilton has been all over the TV screen for the past year or so. She's the incredibly rich, beautiful, and temperamental daughter of Lady Ernestine

Chilton, who got famous years ago for unearthing some pharaoh's tomb. Samantha herself is more famous for her good looks, her partying, her shady boyfriends, and her outrageous antics.

"Ms. Samantha," Q said, *"was Roger Corson's girl-friend at the time he was murdered. For a while police thought that she herself might have killed him. But witnesses saw her on a plane bound for Rome at the time of the murder. She then dropped out of sight before the police could find her to interrogate her.*

"Until the day before yesterday, no one knew where she was. Then Lady Chilton received a troubling phone message. Here, let me play it for you. . . ."

While a slide show of Sam Chilton's greatest poses flashed on the screen, we heard her voice on the phone machine, excited, bubbly, and familiar:

"Mom, hi! It's me—your daughter, Samantha? Remember me? Sorry I've been out of touch, but I had to, like, disappear? 'Cause Roger said it was important. Roger, my boyfriend?

"See, he gave me this map he made? Of the tomb of the Golden Mummy? And he said to take good care of it because it was worth billions and jillions. So I went to Rome and stayed with Pookie and Sly for a week, but then Roger didn't call, and he didn't call, and so I figured, 'Who needs Roger, that jerk? I can find this stupid mummy's tomb myself!'

"So that's what I'm calling to tell you, Mom—you're gonna be so proud of me when I find the tomb and the mummy and the treasure and everything!

"Don't worry, I told the Egyptian Antiquities people, and they said it was okay—in fact, Dr. Mounir himself is coming with me! So is that famous guy, you know, that expert you think is so smart, Dr. Igor Volsky? Oh, and so is Tommy. He's my new boyfriend, and he's totally cute. He was actually Mr. Universe once!

"Oh, yeah . . . about that? If Roger calls, tell him I'm breaking up with him. I can't deal with it when guys never call me. So anyway, we leave the day after tomorrow. And don't worry—I love you, and I'm so excited! Bye! Oh, P.S., I've got a video crew with me to document the whole trip, so you won't miss a thing. It's gonna be the best reality TV show ever! Love you—bye!"

The slide show dissolved back into Q's face. "We have reason to believe that Ms. Chilton really knows nothing of Roger Corson's murder. Lady Chilton tried to reach her daughter, but apparently, she's out of cell phone range. Given everything that's happened, however, Lady C thinks her daughter is in grave danger, and we at ATAC tend to agree."

"Me too," Frank said. "Whoever killed Roger Corson wanted that map, and now she's got it."

"What, you don't think it was the mummy's curse that killed him?"

He gave me a look. Frank doesn't believe in curses. He believes in science, and in hard, cold facts.

"We've traced the phone call to the town of Ras Khalifa, on the Nile," Q said. *"The call came in on the fifteenth. Ms. Chilton says she's leaving 'the day after tomorrow.' That would be the seventeenth."*

"Hey, that's tomorrow!" I realized.

"I know that doesn't leave you boys much time to prepare," Q went on. *"But I have complete confidence in you. Ms. Chilton's boat, the* Ramses II, *leaves the Ras Khalifa dock at seven o'clock in the evening. You must be on the boat with her. Lady Chilton is very worried about her daughter. Your job is to see that no harm comes to her."*

I grabbed the controller and pushed the pause button. "Hey, Frank, how are we supposed to do this? Sam Chilton is never going to let us come along on her expedition—she doesn't know us from a hole in the wall!"

"Why don't we just listen to the rest of what Q has to say?" he suggested. "He usually knows what he's doing, right?"

"I guess so," I said, already thinking ahead. "Ah, yes . . . Sam Chilton and me in the desert, under the stars . . ."

"Don't get too excited, lover boy," Frank said. "She's got her new boyfriend with her, remember?"

"Like that matters? Once she meets me, she'll forget all about him."

"Right," Frank said. "Your muscles are much bigger than Mr. Universe's. Especially the one between your ears."

"Very funny." I pushed play.

"Since Ms. Chilton has been known to never consent to a bodyguard, or even a chaperone, you'll need to have some sort of other cover in order to join the expedition. We've arranged for you to pose as teen reporters for Beautiful People *magazine, doing a feature on the expedition to find the Golden Mummy.*

"As we've all seen, Ms. Chilton cannot resist publicity of any kind. If you play your parts well enough, I'm sure she'll arrange for you to come along."

"Reporters, huh?" I said. "We can do that, right, Frank?"

"Whatever it takes, bro," he said, smiling.

"Your press credentials, notebooks, cameras, cash, plane tickets for tomorrow morning's flight to Ras Khalifa, proper identification, and a few other goodies are in a package being held for you at the hotel desk. You can pick it up anytime."

Q gave us one of his famous cheerless smiles. "Well, boys, that's about it. Good luck. Oh, yes—as usual, this information will obliterate itself in five, four, three, two, one . . ."

The screen went blank, and loud Arabic music blasted out of the speakers.

"Time to get busy," I said, getting up.

"There's just one problem," Frank said.

"Oh, yeah? What's that?"

"How in the world are we going to explain this to Mom and Aunt Trudy?"

3.
A Cruise Down the Nile

Getting permission to go on the expedition turned out to be a piece of cake. In fact, it was the only thing about our entire trip to Egypt that went according to plan.

Dad had already laid the foundation, telling Mom and Trudy how fantastic it was that we'd been hired as "Guest Reporters" by *Beautiful People* magazine and directed to cover Samantha Chilton's search for the Tomb of the Golden Mummy.

Mom, of course, thought it was wonderful that we'd won such a great honor—although she was a little curious about why we hadn't told her weeks ago, when we'd written those essays for the contest about why we wanted to be reporters. In fact, she said, she never even knew we were into journalism!

23

Aunt Trudy, as usual, was not buying into anything without an argument. "I think it's too dangerous," she said as we all ate breakfast at the hotel's buffet. "What if they get lost in the desert? Or bitten by snakes or scorpions? Or attacked by bandits?"

"Well, Trudy," Dad said with a chuckle, "you're welcome to be their chaperone if you like. I can arrange for you to go along."

"*Me?* Oh, no—certainly not," Trudy said, reddening. "I'm not going to rough it at my age."

Which is a joke, really, because Aunt Trudy is as rough and tough as anybody. No snake or scorpion or bandit could stand up to the likes of her. Dad must have known, though, that she'd turn down the offer. She couldn't come with us.

"Besides, I'm sure Playback would miss nesting in my hair," she added with a smirk.

Playback is our pet parrot. The neighbors had been watching him while we were gone, but I knew Trudy didn't trust anyone but herself to take care of her "baby." She had a love/hate relationship with Playback—but it was mostly love.

Trudy still wasn't finished. "And this Samantha Chilton person," she went on. "Isn't she best known as a publicity-hounding hussy? I don't think the boys should get mixed up with her."

"Oh, but Trudy, it's an honor to win first prize in

24

a nationwide essay contest!" Mom argued.

"Honor, my foot! I don't think Frank and Joe should be fooling around with someone so notorious for being bad news."

"Now, Trudy," Mom said, putting a soothing hand on Trudy's arm. "It'll be an incredible educational experience. And I'm sure the boys will behave themselves. Won't you, boys? Promise me and your aunt that you won't do any flirting with Samantha Chilton."

"We promise," we both said.

Then I glanced over at Joe and saw that, behind his back, he had his fingers firmly crossed.

We said good-bye at the airport. Mom, Dad, and Trudy had a long plane trip home to Bayport, and Frank and I had to catch the noon flight to Ras Khalifa, two hundred miles south on the banks of the Nile River, Egypt's lifeline.

Thousands of years ago, when the pharaohs ruled and built their pyramids, most of Egypt's people lived along the Nile. It's no different today. For a few miles on either side of the river, there are towns, farms, and cities. A little farther away from the Nile, there's nothing but desert for thousands of miles.

We could see the lay of the land plainly from the air—*I* could, that is. Joe had his nose buried in the latest issue of *Beautiful People*. One of the main features concerned Samantha Chilton—"The Airhead Heiress," as the magazine called her.

"Listen to this," Joe said excitedly. "'Sam Chilton was seen partying at Nightspot on the Nile yesterday evening. Everyone's wondering who her newest flame is. He sure is a hunk!'"

Joe showed me the magazine. "You think he's a hunk?" he asked, letting me know by his tone that he didn't think so at all.

I studied the picture Joe held out to me. Gorgeously blond Samantha Chilton, in her micromini dancing outfit, was hanging on the arm of a huge blond-haired guy who, I have to admit, didn't look too "hunky" or bright. Still, it was just a photo by some paparazzo—and those pictures can make anyone look bad.

"You're just jealous," I kidded Joe.

"You got that right," he said, taking me seriously.

"Hey, bro," I said, "if you're thinking about using this case as an opportunity to date Samantha Chilton, forget it."

"Forget it? No way! Dating her would be the perfect way to protect her—I'd be with her all the time."

"She's already taken, by the looks of that photo," I reminded him.

"That's only temporary. Ah, yes, I can see it

now—me and Sam, riding double on a camel's back. . . ."

"Dream on, Romeo," I said, laughing. "You'd be better off just treating this as a job. That way, you won't get your heart broken when she rejects you."

"Reject me? Dude, haven't you noticed? I'm irresistible."

I rolled my eyes. "I'm not saying a word."

Ras Khalifa is a dirty, bustling port town, where Nile cruise boats dock for the night, and freighters load and unload. We found the *Ramses II* docked in the harbor, just as Q had promised.

We climbed the wooden ramp and went aboard. A uniformed steward greeted us. "Hello, there," he said, brandishing a clipboard. "Your names, please?"

Joe and I exchanged glances. Q hadn't said anything about putting us on a list.

"We're journalists," I said. "Frank and Joe Hardy, with *Beautiful People* magazine. Here to do a feature on Ms. Chilton."

He looked up and down the list—twice. "I'm so sorry," he said, looking at us as if his heart was breaking. "You are not on the list. Only those on the list are permitted to board."

This was going to be a big problem. We knew we

had to find Samantha Chilton and talk her into taking us along. "Is Ms. Chilton on board yet?" I asked.

The steward looked unsure of himself. "I am not permitted to say."

Aha! That had to mean she was already here. Good.

"Samantha!" I yelled. "Ms. Chilton! HELLO??"

I was taking a chance—a chance that she would hear the racket I was making and come out on deck to see what was happening.

Sure enough, her famous face, framed by that long, sleek, shiny blond hair, leaned over the railing. "Who is that?" she called to the steward. "And why are they screaming my name?"

"We're from the press, Ms. Chilton!" I shouted, flashing the phony press card that came in the package Q sent us.

Come on, fly. Come to the honey.

"*Beautiful People* magazine!" Joe added, giving her his best smile. I glanced over at him and saw that his eyes were glazed over with star worship. He'd had a thing for Samantha Chilton ever since he first saw her on the cover of *People*.

"Ooooh—sounds dreamy!" she said, giggling. "But I'm afraid we're about to sail."

"Could we just talk to you for a minute?" I begged. "They sent us all the way here to Egypt—

we'll get fired if we don't get the story!"

"Gee," she said, looking concerned. "Well, okay, you can come on board—but just for a minute."

Joe and I brushed past the steward and practically ran up the ramp onto the ship.

And what a ship it was! The *Ramses II* was a luxury yacht, built to carry up to fifty people. The decks were polished wood, the railings gleaming brass. Every cabin had a balcony and a picture window, and every detail screamed "first class."

"Sweet!" Joe said, looking around. Then his eyes locked on Samantha Chilton, who, I have to admit, looked even more gorgeous close-up than she did on TV and all those magazine covers.

"Sweet," Joe said again, this time obviously meaning *her*.

Yuck.

We shook hands, and Joe held on to hers way too long.

"The magazine wants us to do a big feature on you and your expedition," I explained. "If it's possible, we'd like to come along for the whole thing."

"Oh. I see. . . . ," she said, knitting her brows. "I'm sorry, but I already have this whole video crew coming."

Joe's face fell as Samantha's brightened. "They're going to tape the whole trip—the opening of the tomb, all the treasures, the mummy and everything—and then they're going to make it into a TV special, and maybe even a reality series!"

"Well," I suggested, "how about if we just concentrate on *you*?"

"Me?"

"Sure! You know, *your* feelings, *your* reactions. Millions of your fans will feel left out if they don't get the 'inside story.'"

She broke into a sudden, sunny smile. "Well, why not? There's always room for more publicity, that's my motto!"

As usual, Q had done his homework—his prediction that Samantha Chilton would invite us aboard had been right on the money.

"Hassan!" she called to the steward, "can you get a cabin made up for these two gentlemen?"

As the steward hustled up the ramp and went off to prepare our cabin, she turned back to us. "Gee, I'm sorry—I don't even know your names!"

"I'm Joe Hardy," Joe said, shaking her hand again, even longer this time. "Oh—and this is my brother, Frank."

"Well, Frank and Joe, welcome aboard. We're gonna have the time of our lives!"

She scrunched up her shoulders, twitched her pretty little nose, and made a happy, excited yip.

I made a mental note to warn Joe again about his crush on Samantha—we couldn't afford to let it get in the way of our job. I could see why Joe found her so irresistible, despite her being such a girly girl—but this was going to be a dangerous mission, and we were going to have to keep our heads—and our hearts—clear.

Just then, the guy from the magazine picture in *Beautiful People* came out on deck and walked over to us. He was blond, at least six foot three, and had muscles like gigantic concrete blocks. He didn't seem happy to see us.

He looked at Joe's hand, still holding Samantha's, and frowned. "What's up?" he asked, in a gruff voice that matched his expression.

"Tommy! Hi, Poopsie!" Samantha gave him a kiss on the cheek, reaching her arms up and around his massive shoulders. "This is Joe Hardy, and this is his brother, Frank. They're reporters—with *Beautiful People* magazine? And they're going to come with us on the expedition, and do a big story all about *me*—isn't that fabu?"

"Yeah. Fabu," said Tommy. He looked at her intently. "You sure about this?" he asked. "We don't need any excess baggage, you know? Besides, you don't know these guys from a hole in the wall."

"Oh, Poopsie," Samantha said, pouting sweetly,

"don't worry—they're from *Beautiful People* magazine! Remember, the more coverage we get for the expedition, the more money we'll get for the TV rights!"

Turning to me and Frank, she added, "Tommy's going to be the executive producer!"

Tommy frowned even more deeply. "I don't know," he said. "If I were you, I'd ditch 'em both—right here, right now."

"Well, you're *not* me," said Samantha, her hands on her hips. She was only about half his weight, and a good six inches shorter, but her personality could have pushed *anybody* around.

"Whatever," Tommy said, backing down and relaxing his hands—they'd been balled up into fists ever since he'd first appeared. "I'll see you back in the cabin."

"Mwah!" Samantha said, blowing a kiss to his retreating figure. "Well, that's that!" she told us, clapping her hands. "Don't worry about Tommy—he's a pussycat once you get to know him."

I wasn't sure I wanted to get to know "Poopsie," pussycat or not.

"He was Mr. Universe a few years ago," she told us. "Isn't that cool?"

"So what is he, like, your bodyguard or something?" Joe asked.

"Bodyguard?" Samantha seemed to think this was a riot. She burst out laughing. "That's a good one—no, he's my boyfriend, actually. Although now that you mention it, I'm going to appoint him my bodyguard, too—he'll love that!"

She walked off down the deck toward her cabin, still laughing. Joe's eyes followed her, disappointed but not defeated.

"That Tommy's a real creep," he said. "I can't believe she'd go for a goon like him."

"I'm sure once she gets to know you, she'll drop him like a hot potato."

I was joking, but once again, Joe didn't get it. "You think so?" he said, flexing his muscles to see how they compared with Tommy's.

They didn't.

"No doubt, bro," I said, clapping him on the back. "I mean, she can't have known him more than a few weeks, right? She was with Roger Corson before that. . . ."

"Hey—I'll bet Tommy's only interested in her because of the treasure!" Joe said.

"Could very well be," I answered. "If Samantha Chilton's in danger, he's definitely a likely suspect. In any case, we've already made ourselves an enemy—and we've only been here ten minutes. Yes, we'll definitely have to keep an eye on 'Poopsie.'"

SUSPECT PROFILE

<u>Name:</u> Tommy "Muscles" McGurk,
a.k.a. "Poopsie"

<u>Hometown:</u> Las Vegas, NV

<u>Physical description:</u> 25 years old, 6' 3", 240 lbs., fair complexion, blond buzz cut, murderous blue eyes, huge muscles, blank look in the eyes.

<u>Occupation:</u> Formerly a bodybuilder, who won the Mr. Universe competition three years ago. Now has no known occupation, other than being Samantha's boyfriend/bodyguard.

<u>Hobby:</u> Breaking concrete walls with his head.

<u>Background:</u> Grew up reading muscle magazines and working out every spare minute. Thinks of his body as a timeless work of art.

<u>Suspicious behavior:</u> The fact that he's going out with Samantha, and going on this expedition, after knowing her only a few weeks at most—and that he doesn't want anyone coming along that he doesn't know. Also, he clearly doesn't like us. That can't be good.

<u>Suspected of:</u> Being a potential danger to Samantha Chilton.

<u>Possible motive:</u> Getting his hands on the Golden Mummy's treasures.

4.

The Mummy Wakes

Frank and I unpacked our suitcases in our cabin. Then we sat on our balcony, sipping cold drinks from our own private, fully stocked minifridge, and watched the sun go down over the desert. The last rays lit up the sails of dozens of feluccas, or small fishing boats, turning them red. These boats had been the chief mode of travel on the Nile for thousands of years.

In fact, if I half-closed my eyes, it could have been the year 3,000 B.C.—during the reign of Pharaoh Semerkhet III, now known as "The Golden Mummy."

Just then, a stretch limo pulled up to the dock—ruining the whole illusion of ancient times—and a uniformed chauffeur got out. He held open the rear door and offered his hand to help a young woman get out.

She didn't take it.

She wore a scarf around her head (a *kaffiyeh*, they call it), dark sunglasses, and a beige cotton robe. It was standard desert dress, but her long, glossy black hair tumbling out from under her scarf made her look very stylish. She looked like she was about twenty years old, at most.

I glanced over at Frank, who was shading his eyes with his hand so he could get a better look at her.

The chauffeur was helping someone else out of the limo now: a big, fat man in a khaki outfit that had to have been custom-made for him. No way do normal shops stock clothes that size.

He also wore dark shades, and a Panama hat topped his enormous head.

"Ah, Dr. Mounir! Welcome, welcome, *Salaam Alaikum*," I heard Hassan say.

"*As Alaikum Salaam*," Dr. Mounir answered. "This is my doctoral assistant, Miss Leila Abdul. She will be traveling with us. Please make up a cabin for her."

"Yes, of course," Hassan said. With a little bow, he led them up the gangplank.

"That must be the guy from the Antiquities Department—you know, the one Sam told her mom about in her phone message," I said.

Frank didn't answer. He was too busy gawking at Leila.

Frank is so pathetic sometimes. He'll tell you that I'm the same way, but it's not true. The difference between us is, I can *handle* myself around girls. Frank goes all to pieces and makes a dork out of himself every time.

Mounir and his pretty assistant were soon out of sight, but down on the dockside, an old, battered taxi was just pulling up. Out of it came a short, thin, bearded man wearing a white linen suit, complete with tie. He wore no hat on his balding head, and his thick glasses reflected back up at me like two setting suns.

If he saw us sitting there, looking down at him, he gave no sign of it. Instead he looked left and right, then skulked quickly up the gangway and onto the ship.

"I wonder who that is," I said.

"Maybe it's that famous Egyptologist Sam Chilton mentioned," Frank guessed. "What was his name again?"

"I forget," I admitted. "Something Russian. But

wasn't that strange, the way he kind of snuck on board? Especially since we came up against that roadblock?"

Frank shrugged. "Maybe he's going to look for the steward," he said. "Let's lie low, make a note of it, and see what we can find out later."

As the sky grew dark and the stars came out, the *Ramses II* weighed anchor, and we set off on our journey up the Nile, toward the south.

"Well," I said to Frank. "What do you say we go meet our fellow travelers and find something to eat?"

"Sounds good to me."

We went toward the stern of the ship and down a flight of stairs. The lower deck held a large dining room area. Looking in through the picture windows, we could see that the video team had set up their lights for taping.

When it looked like they were between takes, Frank and I stepped inside. Once my eyes adjusted to the glare, I could make out Tommy sitting in the dark shadows, off to one side. I turned my attention back to the "set." A man we hadn't seen before sat in a chair on one side. He was good-looking in a rugged sort of way, about thirty years old, with long, carefully brushed brown hair. He wore a stylish short-sleeved shirt and khakis. On his lap was a clipboard with notes.

Four people sat facing him in a row: Dr. Mounir, his assistant Leila, Sam Chilton, and the little bald man with the beard we'd seen sneaking onto the ship. Since he was sitting there with everyone else, I guessed he hadn't really been sneaking. Still, the way he'd slipped on board was weird.

He looked nervous now, scared. He was holding a drink in his hand, and it was shaking enough to make the ice cubes tinkle.

A roly-poly guy with a buzz cut adjusted a boom mike that hung over the panelists' heads, just out of camera range.

The cameraman was busy adjusting his focus. He had a halo of long, wild, curly red hair.

"Quiet on the set!" the guy with the boom mike said.

"And, rolling," said the cameraman. "Take three, and . . . action!"

The interviewer said, "Tell me, Dr. Mounir—what is your job on this expedition?"

The fat man smiled. "I shall watch over and catalog all the treasures we find, to make sure that they are not stolen, broken, or mishandled. These treasures shall forever belong to all the Egyptian people, as a part of their glorious heritage."

"What about you, Dr. Volsky?" the interviewer asked, turning to the little man with the beard.

"I am here to verify the authenticity of all the objects as we unearth them," he said. "I will also place them in context—that is, describe their relationship to each other, and to their time in history."

"Dr. Volsky is the world's biggest expert on this stuff," Sam Chilton interrupted. "I'm so excited he's coming with us! Between him and Dr. Mounir, and *you*, Theo," she added, giving the interviewer a flirty look, "everything we do will be carefully recorded for future generations!" She gave a little squeak of delight and clapped her hands together.

I saw Leila's mouth twitch slightly in disgust. It was clear that she didn't like Sam. Was it just because Sam was a flirt? Maybe what Leila didn't like was that Sam was making a circus out of the search for the Golden Mummy's Tomb.

"And what about the so-called Curse of the Golden Mummy?" Theo asked. He had a slight European accent, but I wasn't sure what kind.

Dr. Mounir grew solemn and nodded his head slowly. "Ah, yes, the curse. I think we must all be very careful, lest we disrespect the dead. Who knows what powers the ancients had, or still have?

I do not think it is crazy to believe in such things as curses."

Dr. Volsky snickered. "Ridiculous," he said.

"I beg your pardon?" Dr. Mounir said, his eyes growing wide.

"Utterly absurd," Dr. Volsky insisted. "These stories of curses are nothing more than fairy tales! We must stick to science, and only science!"

Dr. Mounir's eyes blazed with anger. "Do not forget, my esteemed friend," he said, "that after the discovery of King Tutankhamen's tomb, so many of the expedition's members died . . . mysteriously."

"Pure coincidence," said Dr. Volsky.

"I wonder," said Theo.

"There is more in this world than your modern science can explain," said Dr. Mounir, his eyes narrowing to little slits.

"I, for one, am not afraid of such curses," said Dr. Volsky.

"Oh no? Then why are your hands shaking?" Dr. Mounir asked.

"Just a reflex!" Volsky replied, both hands gripping his glass tightly so they wouldn't shake anymore.

"What about you, Ms. Abdul?" Theo broke in, trying to head off the argument—or maybe encourage

41

it. "What do you think about curses?"

"I believe in respecting the dead," she said seriously. "I believe in respecting our history and our culture. The ancients have much to teach us, if we are humble enough to listen."

"Ah," said Theo, "very wise, very wise."

From the darkness, I heard Tommy snicker.

"Cut!" said the cameraman. "Let's do another take. I picked up a noise."

"People," said Theo, "please! We need complete quiet here, or we'll be doing this all night. You'll all have a chance to give your opinions."

"Perhaps Tommy should just wait outside, Theo?" Sam suggested.

"Good idea," said Theo.

"You don't want me around? Fine!" Tommy got up, threw his chair to the ground, and stormed out of the room. "I'm only the executive producer. . . ."

"You'll have to forgive him," Sam told the rest of us. "He's not used to foreign customs."

"Foreign customs?" Leila repeated, getting to her feet. "You mean, like being polite? Being humble? Having manners?" She stomped off, leaving the dining room on the opposite side of the deck from Tommy.

"I guess we'll have to break for the night," Theo

said with a sigh of frustration. "Nels, you can pack away the camera. Jurgen, you get the lights and the sound equipment. We'll set up on shore in the morning."

"Mummies' curses. Ridiculous!" muttered Dr. Volsky as he got up, still clutching his drink. "Humbug!"

"Oh, come on now, Dr. Volsky," Samantha said with a musical laugh. "You sound just like a Scrooge!"

"A what?"

"Scrooge. You know. . . ."

"I have no idea what you are talking about," Volsky said as Sam led him out on deck.

Clearly, he was not a believer in things mysterious. I guess you can't be, if you make a habit of opening mummies' tombs.

It was obvious to me, though, that he was scared of *something*.

Frank and I went back to our cabin and sat out on deck, watching the dark shore go by.

"So, what did you think of all that?" I asked.

"It was kind of tense."

"Totally. Did you see the way Tommy threw that chair down?"

"Yeah. He's got a real chip on his shoulder,"

Frank agreed. "It's like he's ready to kill anyone who flirts with his girlfriend."

"That guy, Theo?"

"Samantha sure seemed friendly with him."

"I'll say."

"Mounir and Volsky almost got into it too," Frank said.

"Did you notice Volsky's hands shaking?"

"How could you not?"

"And that Leila chick. She can't stand Sam," I observed.

"Oh, it's 'Sam' now? Aren't we getting friendly? If our friend Tommy thinks you have designs on her . . ."

"He already thinks I have designs on her," I said.

"Do you?"

"Are you kidding me? Of course I do!"

"Better take it easy there, Tiger. It could be a dangerous game," Frank warned.

"Hey, bro, never mind that musclehead—we've got a mummy's curse to worry about."

"You believe that?" he asked.

I thought for a minute. "I'm not sure. One thing I *am* sure of is that Leila Abdul can't stand Sam Chilton."

"And why do you think that is?"

I shrugged. "Jealous, maybe?"

"Or maybe it's because some bratty rich girl comes over here with her millions and barges in on what should be an Egyptian-led adventure."

"Oooh! Do I detect a note of righteous anger?" I asked. "Don't tell me you have a crush on Dr. Mounir's lovely assistant?"

Even though it was dark, I could tell Frank was blushing.

"Cut it out," he muttered. "I'm just defending her, that's all. I happen to agree, up to a point. And you have to admit, she's got fire, and brains. . . ."

"And she's not bad-looking, either," I added.

"Would you stop it? I happen to agree with her point about being culturally sensitive, that's all."

"Me too," I said. "But I still say she's a babe. So's Sam Chilton. And I think we should get to know them both a whole lot better."

"Joe . . ."

"You know—for the sake of our mission."

It was getting late, and we were both totally beat. We got ready for bed and were halfway to dreamland when a piercing scream brought us both back to full alertness.

It came from the direction of Sam Chilton's cabin.

We ran for all we were worth. The door to Sam's cabin was wide open. She was inside—alive, thank goodness. She looked shaken up, though.

"What happened?" I asked, taking her gently by the shoulders. "Are you okay?"

"I'm fine," she said. "I mean, no! I'm not fine. You wouldn't be fine either, if you'd just been knocked down by a mummy!"

5.
Things Start to Unravel

At first I thought she was joking. I'd read in the tabloids that Samantha Chilton had pulled off some pretty extreme pranks in her time. But she seemed really scared—her face was ghostly white, and she was shaking all over.

"Calm down," Joe told her, holding her firmly by the shoulders and leaning his forehead against hers. "Take a deep breath. That's it."

Samantha had her eyes closed, but she was still shaking like a leaf.

"You'd better sit down," Joe said, "and tell us what happened."

She sat on the edge of her bed, and Joe sat next to her, his arm around her shoulders, comforting her.

Just as I was thinking what Tommy would do if he saw the two of them like that, he burst in through the door. With a roar, he grabbed Joe, yanked him to his feet, lifted him up, and shook him like a rag doll.

"What did you do to my girl?" he yelled. "I swear I'll tear you from limb to limb if you hurt her!"

"Tommy, stop it!" Samantha shouted. "Leave him alone—he was just trying to help me."

"Yeah, right. Keep your hands off her," he told Joe before throwing him across the cabin.

Joe landed hard. "Ow!" he said. "Hey, what'd I ever do to you?"

"Did he hurt you?" Tommy asked her, ignoring Joe.

"They just came in here because I screamed," she tried to explain.

"Why'd you scream?"

"Because there was a *mummy* in here!" she said, getting all riled up again.

"A *what*?"

"A mummy! A mummy! What are you, deaf?"

"What do you mean, a mummy?" Tommy asked.

"I was up at the front of the ship, trying to get a cell phone signal so I could call my mom. Of course I couldn't get through—it's just one big dead zone around here."

Dr. Volsky's head peered around the side of the door, followed by Theo's. "What's going on?" Theo asked.

Dr. Mounir appeared, and Leila, Nels, and Jurgen followed, crowding into the doorway.

"There," Joe told Sam. "*Everybody's* here now. You can just tell the story once and be done with it."

"I came back here to the cabin, and my door was locked. And I thought, 'That's funny, they only lock from the inside.' And just as I was about to go get the steward, the door opens, and this . . . this *thing* is standing there! I started screaming, and it knocked me over and ran."

"Which way did it go?" Theo asked.

"I don't know . . . that way, I think," she said, pointing toward the stern. "But I'm not really sure. I was just so scared. . . ."

"Did you chase after the mummy?" Leila asked her.

"Are you kidding me? Would *you* have? I'm telling you, I was totally terrified. I still am!"

"We know," Volsky said. "We all heard the scream."

"Well, there's a *mummy* on this boat," Samantha said. "You'd have screamed too if you saw him!"

"Listen," Dr. Volsky said, "you're overtired. You probably had a bad dream that seemed very real—"

"I did *not* have a dream!" Samantha insisted. "I was wide awake! Doesn't anybody here believe me? Dr. Mounir, you believe in mummies, right?"

Mounir looked embarrassed. "I do indeed—but the ones I have seen with my own eyes have always been as still as the grave."

"You said yourself, there are mummies' curses!"

"Yes. And I believe it is true that you saw the mummy, Ms. Chilton, but perhaps it was only in your mind—perhaps you have been sent this vision because the Golden Mummy's spirit does not want foreigners to enter his burial chamber. Perhaps you should stay behind and allow Egyptians to lead the expedition to uncover the tomb."

Was Mounir taking advantage of Samantha to get what he wanted?

Samantha put her hands to her head and screamed again. "It was *not* a vision! It was a *real mummy*—it knocked me down, for goodness' sake! Why does nobody believe me?!"

"All right, all right," Tommy said. "We'll go search the ship. If there's a mummy on board, we'll find him for you. And I'll snap his neck like a twig!"

"It won't help," Joe said. "Mummies are already dead."

Tommy's lip curled menacingly. "I don't care," he said, giving Joe a warning look. "Nobody messes with my girlfriend. Nobody, alive or dead."

"Thank you, Poopsie," Samantha told Tommy. "But somebody's got to stay with me—I can't be alone in here, and I'm not going searching for that . . . that *thing*!"

"I'll stay with you," Joe offered.

"Not a chance, pal," Tommy said, stepping between him and Samantha. "I'll stay with her. *You* go search."

"Whatever," Joe said, knowing better than to argue with a former Mr. Universe who'd already shown us what he could do to people he disliked.

"Come on, everybody," I said. "Let's break into groups and search the whole ship. Check every cabin, every closet."

Leila, Mounir, and Volsky took the bow. Theo and his video crew went down below, to the crew's quarters and the engine room. Joe and I headed toward the stern, where Sam had last seen the so-called mummy.

We checked every cabin along the way. As Samantha had noticed, the doors to the cabins locked only from the inside, and they were all empty, since everyone was out searching for the mummy.

"You've really made a friend in Tommy," I joked, opening a door and peeking inside.

But Joe didn't laugh. "Hey, Frank, you don't

believe in this mummy story of hers, do you?"

I looked around, found nothing, and shut the door. "I don't believe in walking, talking mummies who knock women down, no. But *somebody* was in that cabin, nosing around."

"Oh, yeah? How do you know? It didn't look ransacked or anything."

"No," I agreed, continuing on to the next door. "Whoever went through it was being careful. They took the trouble to dress like a mummy, so that if they got caught, they could get away without their identity being revealed."

"But who could it have been?" Joe wondered.

"Anyone," I said. "Everyone was in his or her cabin, supposedly."

"So somebody wraps up to look like a mummy, in case he or she is caught?"

"That's right."

"You think someone on the ship is after Roger Corson's map?" he asked.

"Exactly. That map has to be in Samantha's cabin. If someone got their hands on it, they could beat everyone else to the tomb and make off with the entire treasure!"

"Do you think the criminal found it?"

"No, or the mummy would have been gone by the time Sam came back."

We were at the stern now. "Sam's cabin is pretty near the bow," Joe said. "So it makes sense that the mummy would run this way. More places to hide."

"There's another reason," I said.

"Oh, yeah? What's that?"

"They had to get rid of the wrapping."

"The wrapping?"

"Joe, if you want to dress up like a mummy, you need a whole lot of gauze."

"Riiight . . . ," Joe said, getting it. "So they came back here, knowing everyone would be rushing to Sam's cabin. And they tossed the wrapping overboard, so there wouldn't be any proof of Sam's story."

"Exactly."

"Well, then, there's not much point in our staying back here, is there?"

"No. Unless . . ."

"Unless they didn't toss it far enough," Joe finished for me. He leaned over the railing, peering down in the darkness. "Hey . . . I think I see something down there!"

He climbed over the railing and lowered himself over the other side.

"Hey! Be careful!" I shouted after him as he dangled, swinging back and forth until he dropped down on the edge of the lower deck, where the crew had their quarters. Then he reached over that railing and down toward the water.

Something was trailing off a hook that protruded from the back of the ship, near the exhaust pipe.

Something white, streaming out into the black water.

Joe reeled it in and held it up for me to see. "Gauze!" he shouted.

So much for the live mummy theory.

We took our find back to show the others. They had already finished their searches and had found nothing.

"So it wasn't a real mummy after all," Samantha said, her hands on her hips.

She had really been scared when she thought there was a real mummy around. But no mere human wrapped in gauze was going to keep Sam Chilton from being the first to find the Golden Mummy's tomb and getting all the televised glory for herself.

"Well," said Dr. Mounir, "I see that in this case, you are correct. It was not a mummy, for sure, but a live human being. That does not mean, however, that there is no mummy's curse."

"Mummy's curse? Yeah, right," Tommy said. "Ha! What a load of baloney! I'll bet *you're* the one who did it, just to scare us into calling off the expedition!"

"That is an outrageous accusation!" Dr. Mounir shouted, pointing a fat finger skyward. "I demand a full apology!"

"No way!" Tommy shot back.

"Apologize to Dr. Mounir, Tommy," Sam demanded.

"Huh?"

"It wasn't him, I'm sure of that."

"How do you know?" Tommy asked. "It could have been anybody, since everyone was in their own cabin."

"Yes," Dr. Mounir agreed, glaring at Tommy. "Even you, sir."

"It wasn't Dr. Mounir," Samantha repeated. "I'd have known. There aren't too many—ahem—chubby mummies."

Dr. Mounir made a face, then glared at everyone—especially me and Joe. Clearly, he was unhappy about the attention. He had tried to convince Sam Chilton to give up the expedition and to let *him* uncover the mummy's tomb himself—and now everyone was putting the pieces together. Not just us.

Joe and I, it seemed, had just made another enemy. And even if Mounir wasn't the one who'd broken into Sam's cabin, he might still have been behind it.

SUSPECT PROFILE

Name: Dr. Fayez Mounir

Hometown: Cairo, Egypt

Physical description: 50 years old, 5' 10", 320 lbs.

Occupation: Head of the Egyptian Ministry of Antiquities, he's been a government official all his adult life. He does incredibly well on his modest government salary—lives in a mansion, dresses in five-thousand-dollar suits, and is driven around in a stretch limo by a uniformed chauffeur.

Hobby: Getting himself onto TV talk shows as an expert.

Background: Grew up getting picked on in his school because he was fat. But he showed them all—he went further in life than any of those thin kids. Living well is the best revenge, and to Dr. Mounir, revenge is thousand-calorie sweet.

Suspicious behavior: He keeps trying to get Sam Chilton to back out of this expedition. All the talk of mummies' curses seems designed to scare everyone away.

Suspected of: Trying to get all the glory—and maybe the mummy's treasure—for himself.

Possible motive: Mounir wants the glory. Plain and simple.

The next morning Joe and I woke up with the sun streaming through the curtains of our cabin. Our ship had already docked, and porters were busy unloading the tents, food, and other goods that would be traveling into the desert with us on the backs of our camels.

The camels were lined up below, just beyond the dock. Workers were strapping bundles of food, tents, video equipment, and other tools onto their backs.

Soon we, too, would be riding on those strong backs, into the empty desert that began just a few miles from the river's edge.

Everyone was shouting. Foremen barked orders to the porters, the porters yelled at each other, passersby offered advice at the tops of their lungs.

Theo, Nels, and Jurgen were videotaping the entire scene. I had to admit, this would definitely make a cool opening scene for a reality TV show.

Over to one side of the row of camels, Samantha was standing with Tommy. He was checking off the names of the workmen on his clipboard, and Sam was paying them with wads of Egyptian money.

Joe and I got washed and dressed, packed up what little we had unpacked, and headed down the gangplank to join the commotion.

By the time we got to Samantha and Tommy, they were into yet another argument with Dr. Mounir. This time it seemed to be a fight over which workmen were going to be hired for our journey.

"No," Mounir was saying, "I cannot allow those men to join the expedition." He pointed to a group of six young men in *jellabias*, the long, white garments reaching down to the knees that several of the locals wore. "They have not been cleared by government security. These are very sensitive treasures we are talking about. Not just anyone is fit to handle them."

"And you think *those* guys are more trustworthy?" Tommy asked, pointing to another group of men standing behind Dr. Mounir.

This group looked a lot less shipshape than the first bunch. One had a long scar going all the way down the side of his face. Another wore a black eye patch. All six of them wore long, curved knives in their belts, and they looked as if they would kill you as soon as look at you.

"These men are from my personal staff," Dr. Mounir assured Samantha and Tommy. "You can trust them with your very lives."

"Thanks, but I'll pass on that," Tommy muttered.

Joe and I were standing about thirty feet away. Suddenly Dr. Volsky appeared beside us. I guess he'd been watching the argument too.

"I don't trust that fellow," he muttered, loud enough for us to hear him.

"Who? Dr. Mounir?" I asked.

Volsky nodded. "I've known him for years, of course. He forced the old director of antiquities out and brought in his own team. None of them are experts in the field, mind you—but all are completely loyal to him."

"Are you saying he's corrupt?" Joe asked.

Volsky let out a bitter laugh. "I don't have to say it. He reeks of corruption, and everyone in the field knows it. He makes only a modest salary, yet he lives in a fantastic mansion and has chauffeurs to drive him everywhere. Mark my words: Ms. Chilton will rue the day she agreed to let him come along on this expedition."

"Seems to me like she didn't have much choice," I said.

He grunted. "Perhaps not. But she will be sorry nevertheless. Dr. Mounir is up to something evil, mark my words." With that, he walked away to inspect the row of camels.

"You know," Joe said, "I have to agree with the little guy. Those camel drivers of Mounir's look like a bunch of thugs."

"You noticed," I said. "Yep, I think we'd better stay extra alert. Mummy's curse or not, I've got a funny feeling that Sam Chilton's in real danger here."

6.
Into the Desert

I didn't like the looks of this showdown, and neither did Frank. Our job was to protect Sam Chilton, and Dr. Mounir's six guys looked like they were ready to strike.

From the bits of conversation we could hear (lots of it was in Arabic, between the newly hired crew and Mounir), it seemed like two of the men were desert guides, three were porters to lift and carry all our heavy gear, and one was going to be our cook.

Just when it seemed like things were wrapping up, a tall, thin man in a jellabia stepped forward. He had a long beard, and wore a white kaffiyeh headdress.

"Please, madam!" he shouted as he approached the group on the dock. "I am Ahmed, the Happy Hippie! I am here to guide you into the desert!"

"No, thanks, pal," Tommy said, stepping between the Happy Hippie and Sam. "We've already got our guides lined up."

"Those two?" Ahmed said with a laugh. "They do not know how to find the back end of a donkey!"

The two men he was pointing at reached for their knives, but Tommy took charge before things got out of hand. "These are official guides from the Egyptian Ministry of Antiquities," he told the disappointed Ahmed.

Suddenly the Happy Hippie smiled again. "I will be your cook, then!" he shouted, clapping his hands and doing a little dance that made Sam laugh.

None of Mounir's men even smiled. They looked at Ahmed suspiciously, and why not? This guy had come out of nowhere—literally—and was trying to mess up the sweet deal their boss had just rammed down Sam Chilton's throat.

"We've got our cook, too," Tommy said, pointing to the guy Mounir had brought in for that purpose.

"Him? I can see that his hands have never even made hummus!" Ahmed said. "Have you tried his cooking?"

"My cooking is the best in all of Egypt!" the accused man shot back. His hand reached for the handle of his knife, ready for action.

"Then you must taste it and decide for yourselves!" Ahmed told Tommy and Sam. "Afterward, you shall taste mine, and then we shall see whose is better."

"We don't have time for that," Tommy insisted. "We're getting ready to leave now."

"It is all right," Mounir's chosen cook said. "I have some of my famous hummus right here."

He reached into his sack and took out a covered plastic bowl and some pita bread. He put them down and reached back into the sack. "I know I've got a spoon in here somewhere," he muttered.

The entire group was watching him try to find the spoon. Meanwhile, unnoticed by everyone (except me and Frank, who were standing right behind him), Ahmed reached into his pocket and pulled out a small pouch. Kneeling down, partly hidden by the other man's robe, he sprinkled some white powder onto the hummus when no one was looking. Our "Happy Hippie" was an accomplished cheater.

"Here," Mounir's cook said, picking up the bowl and passing it to Sam along with a piece of the bread. "Try my famous hummus for yourself!"

Sam reached for the bread and dipped it into the hummus.

"No!" I shouted. "Sam—wait!"

It had all happened so fast—and I hadn't acted quickly enough. By the time I shouted my warning, Sam had already tasted the hummus.

Was I too late? Would she drop dead right there on the dock, poisoned by this sinister stranger?

Sam made a face. "Yuck!" she said, spitting once or twice just to get rid of the aftertaste. "That is the most awful crud I've ever tasted!"

"What?" the cook said, astonished. "Here, let me taste that." He tried it, and spat it out just as Sam had. "Something is wrong," he said, confused.

"Now try mine!" Ahmed said. "I happen to have some here. I packed my own lunch—you must try it and see!"

He offered some to Sam. She seemed not to want to taste something that looked exactly like the stuff she'd just spat out.

"Please, just try it!" Ahmed urged.

"This is an outrage!" said Dr. Mounir, his face going red. "I have eaten Salim's cooking for years, and it is always the best!"

"Mmmmm!" Sam said, tasting Ahmed's hummus. "This is delicious—it's amazing! What a difference!"

"I swear, mine tasted fine this morning!" Salim protested, but it was too late.

"You're fired, dude," Tommy told him.

"Excuse me," Dr. Mounir interrupted. "But we have just agreed—"

"Too bad," Tommy told him. "Sam's still the boss of this expedition, and if she likes the Happy Hippie's cooking, that's who we're hiring."

Still grumbling, Salim grabbed his sack and stormed off down the street. Ahmed, now a *truly* happy hippie, shook Tommy's and Sam's hands. "Thank you, thank you," he said, bowing over and over again. "You will not be sorry, I promise you." Tommy gave Ahmed some money, they talked for a bit, and Ahmed took off—I guessed to buy some groceries.

"I'm already sorry," I said to Frank. "Did you see the stunt that guy just pulled?"

"I did," Frank said.

"Maybe we should have blown the whistle on him?"

"What, and eat that other guy's food? At least we know Ahmed's is good. And hey, at least it wasn't poison. Must have been something like baking powder." He paused for a second, then said, "Samantha would be dead by now."

"You got that right," I said. "What a relief! If it *had* been poison . . ."

"Well," Frank said, "next time, we'll just have to react quicker."

"If there *is* a next time."

"Oh, don't worry. There will be."

"What makes you so sure?"

"I don't know," Frank said. "But there's a whole lot of treasure at stake here, not to mention national pride, and maybe even something supernatural. I'm betting this trip we're about to take is going to be dangerous with a capital D."

Late that afternoon, when the extreme heat of the day was past and Ahmed had returned with boxes full of groceries for our trip, our caravan set off westward into the great Sahara desert. We rode on camels (and boy, are they ever a bumpy ride!). My rear end was hurting after the first fifteen minutes, so I wasn't thrilled about the prospect of being on camelback for days and days.

The guides and porters were riding two to a camel, while the rest of us each had our own ride.

Each camel also carried saddlebags full of food, water, and gear. They are strong beasts, let me tell you, and they almost never need water. I don't know how they do it. I was hitting the water bottle every ten minutes or so. Even this late in the day, the temperature had to be over ninety degrees.

"We need to get closer to Sam," said Frank as we rode side by side. "Otherwise, we won't be able to stop the next attempt on her life."

We spurred our camels and caught up to Sam. Frank asked, "Ms. Chilton, do you think we could do an interview with you while we ride?"

"Oh, sure thing!" she said, giving us a smile that nearly made me fall off my camel. Man, was she gorgeous!

"Do you want to tape it? I can get Theo to set up a handheld camera and some mikes. . . ."

"That won't be necessary," Frank said.

"And could we, you know . . . talk to you in private?" I added.

She gave us a puzzled look. "In private? What for?"

"Well," I explained, "you know . . . you might want to share some . . . intimate details for our readers. Stuff that not everybody needs to hear, especially before the article gets published."

"Oh, I get it!" she said. "You're afraid of being scooped!"

"Right!" I said.

"But there aren't any other reporters around here."

"You never know," I told her, indicating our companions. "Any magazine can hire someone and pay them to get information."

"So why should I trust *you*?"

I was suddenly speechless. Thank goodness Frank came to my rescue.

"We found that gauze wrapping last night, didn't we?" he pointed out. "That should prove to you that we're on your side. Besides, look at that face," he said, meaning mine. "Is that the face of a liar?"

It *was*, actually—I mean, I was here pretending to be a reporter. I'd never even written for the *Bayport High School Gazette*!

But Samantha seemed to think my face was innocent enough. "Okay," she said. "Public or private, what do I care? Everybody knows everything about me anyway."

Well, not exactly, I thought. But we were going to do our best to find out.

We dropped back behind the rest of the party, out of hearing distance.

"So," Sam said, "what do you want to know?"

"Well, first of all," I said, "tell us about you and Tommy. How did you meet? Weren't you with someone else just a month ago?"

"Yeah," she said with a sigh. "I really loved Roger too. But he kind of blew me off—told me to get lost and not call him for a while. And he was acting all nervous, but he wouldn't share his feelings with me. Typical man, huh?"

"Uh, yeah," I said, just to keep her going.

"He did share something *else* with you, though, didn't he?" Frank asked.

"How'd you know that?" Sam squinted at him—the setting sun was shining right in our faces, but that wasn't why. She was suspicious of us, and that was not a good thing.

"How did we know that? We're reporters!" Frank explained. "It's our job to find out things. That's how we know about the map."

Sam gasped, and her eyes widened. "How did you know that? I never told *anyone* about that! Well, except for Tommy . . . and my mother . . . and maybe one or two other people. I forget . . . no, no—I'm *sure* that was it."

"Do you still have the map?" I asked.

"Of course I do!" she said, giving me a sly smile. "Do you think we'd still be going on this trip if that mummy had taken the map from my cabin?"

"So the intruder didn't find the map?" Frank asked.

"No—because it wasn't in the cabin," she said, pleased with herself. "I keep it on me at all times, see. That way, nobody can take it without me knowing."

"That doesn't guarantee they won't *try*," I pointed out.

"Let them," she said. "I'm not scared. Tommy can protect me."

Frank cleared his throat. "About Tommy," he said. "How long have you known the guy?"

"Oh, a *long* time," she said. "Almost three weeks."

"Three weeks!" I exclaimed. "How do you know you can trust him?"

"My first impressions of people are always right," she said.

"Really?" I asked. "Um, and what's your first impression of . . . me, say?"

She looked me up and down, smiling. "You're really cute," she said.

I lost my balance and nearly fell backward off my camel. "Really?"

"Uh-huh."

"Ms. Chilton," Frank interrupted, "I hate to say this, but Joe and I think you may be in great danger."

"*Me?* Why?" she said, forgetting all about how cute I was. Sometimes I could just kill Frank.

"The map," he reminded her.

"Oh. Right," she said. "But Dr. Mounir's here with us, and all his men—so the Egyptian government can protect me."

"Uh, well, sort of," I put in. "Except there are

70

some people who seem to think Dr. Mounir's not altogether . . . honest."

"You mean Dr. Volsky?" Sam said, waving a hand in the air. "Oh, don't pay any attention to him. Igor's just jealous. He *wishes* he had a big government job like Dr. Mounir's."

"That might be true," I said. "But it doesn't mean he isn't right about Mounir. After all, whoever wants that map has already killed once to get it."

"What?"

That got her attention.

"Who? Who's been killed?"

Q had been right. How had she not heard the news? Maybe it was because she was traveling—or maybe she wasn't that into learning about world events.

Frank cleared his throat again. "I'm afraid I have bad news, Ms. Chilton. Roger Corson was murdered the night after you left London. A man—or woman—dressed as a mummy was seen fleeing the apartment."

Now it was Sam's turn to lose her balance. "Oh, my . . . ," she whispered. "And last night—that mummy in my cabin . . . !"

"You're lucky to be alive, Ms. Chilton," Frank said.

71

"Poor Roger! And I thought he didn't call me in Rome because he didn't want to be my boyfriend anymore!"

She was crying now, the tears making tracks down her beautiful cheeks.

"I'm sure he cared about you a whole lot," Frank said. "Otherwise, he wouldn't have given you the map of the Golden Mummy's tomb."

"That's t-true," she said, still crying. "He did say it was very important, and not to tell anyone. But when I didn't hear from him, I decided he was a total jerk, and that I'd go dig up the tomb myself. Now I feel just *awful*!"

"Tell us more about Tommy. How did you meet him?"

"It was at a club—Nightspot on the Nile. We were introduced, and it was, like, love at first sight. And when I told him I was going to go on this expedition, he said he was coming too, and that was that!"

"So you don't know a thing about him, really," I said.

"That's not true. I know he was Mr. Universe a few years ago."

"And what else?" I asked.

"Um . . . . listen, he's a very nice person, and I trust him totally," she insisted. "To-tal-ly."

72

"Okay, okay," Frank said. "But it's still important for you to be careful. *Somebody* on this expedition wants that map of yours badly enough to kill for it. Like my brother told you, they've already killed once to get it."

Sam put her hand to her chest, taking it all in. Then she took a deep breath and stuck her chin out bravely. "I'm not backing down," she said. "For poor Roger's sake, I'm going to find this treasure and give it all to the Egyptian people. That's what he would have wanted. And if anyone tries to stop me—well, just let them try!"

I had to hand it to her—she was brave. But that alone was not going to be enough to keep Sam Chilton alive.

"May I make a suggestion?" Frank asked. "Tonight, when you go to sleep, have Theo and his crew set up a closed-circuit camera outside your tent. That way, if anyone tries any monkey business, we'll catch them in the act."

"Good idea," she said. "I'll do that." She thought for a minute. "You guys are really reporters?"

"*Beautiful People* magazine," I said. "Yup—we're the real deal."

"Huh. You're not like any reporters I've ever met. You guys are so much more together."

"Thanks," I said.

"Ms. Chilton," Frank said, "when all this is over, we'll write your story for all the world to hear. But first, we need you to come through this expedition alive. From here on in, just remember—you're in great danger, every minute of the day or night. *Especially* the night."

Sam nodded her head slowly. "I'll remember that," she said. "Thanks." Then she spurred her camel and took off in pursuit of the others.

"That was a great idea about the video link," I said. "But do you really think that'll stop whoever it is from trying to steal the map?"

"No way," Frank admitted. "But at least we'll get them on tape. They'll have one more try at Sam, and that will be their last chance."

"Right," I said. "And we'll be ready for them too."

7.
Night of the Dead

We didn't make camp until well after sunset. The first stars were coming out over the desert, and the mountains of sand were fading into blackness.

Dr. Mounir's handpicked crew of men went to work, pitching tents and building a fire, while the rest of us pretty well collapsed from exhaustion. We found comfortable spots to sit under the palm trees surrounding the small water hole where we'd stopped for the night.

Samantha went over to talk to Theo. I guessed she was asking him to set up the closed-circuit camera we'd advised. He nodded his head, looking serious, then went rummaging through his metal equipment boxes to find all the necessary stuff.

Meanwhile, Dr. Mounir was munching on a bunch of dates his men had picked off a palm tree for him, and telling stories to whoever would listen—namely Leila, Nels, Jurgen, Dr. Volsky, and Ahmed the Happy Hippie, who was also busy getting everyone's dinner ready.

"It wasn't just Tutankhamen's tomb," Mounir was saying. "After Amenhotep IV's tomb was violated, all the members of the expedition died— horrible, unexplainable deaths, one after the other."

"That doesn't mean there was a mummy's curse," Dr. Volsky protested.

"And it doesn't mean there wasn't," Mounir shot back. "Am I not correct, Leila?"

Leila looked down at the ground. It was impossible to know what she thought about anything, but I could see that she was uncomfortable being asked to speak in front of such famous company. "Whatever you say, Doctor," she mumbled.

"There, you see? She agrees with me!" Mounir bellowed, slapping his knee for emphasis and eating another big mouthful of dates.

"It's all hogwash," Dr. Volsky insisted. "You're supposed to be a scientist, Mounir, so be scientific! Once you die, you stay dead—you don't come back to life and kill people. If those explorers died

violently, it must have been at the hands of someone living, not dead."

"I'll tell you what," Nels spoke up. "I'm getting
the willies just thinking about it."

"Me too," Jurgen agreed. "Can't we change the
subject?"

"I wish it were that simple," Dr. Mounir said
with a sigh. "But here we all are, ready to repeat the
same mistakes that cost those explorers their lives."

"Well, what are we supposed to do?" Tommy
asked. "Turn back now, after we've come this far?"

"It is not too late," Dr. Mounir said seriously.
"In the interests of science, I will go forward alone,
with my men and with my trusted assistant."

He put a hand on Leila's shoulder, and I saw her
stiffen. "We will discover what is there, and we will
leave it in place, respecting the dead and our glorious history."

"No way," Tommy said. "If it weren't for Sam,
you wouldn't even know this stupid tomb had
been discovered. You're just lucky she's already
rich and doesn't care about keeping all the treasure
for herself."

The air was thick with tension until Ahmed
clapped his hands, and everybody nearly jumped
three feet in the air.

"The mummy says 'fill your tummy'!" he announced. Everyone started laughing at him, and just like that, the tension was broken.

Ahmed pranced around, imitating a mummy—he looked more like a clown, really—and then proceeded to serve us the most delicious meal Joe and I'd had so far in Egypt: lamb cubes roasted over an open fire, with hummus and marinated salad on the side.

The stars came out in their trillions—the most I'd ever seen—and pretty soon we were all feeling much, much better.

Everyone was tired to the bone. Even Samantha, who always seemed to have more energy than anybody else, was yawning. It was time to turn in for the night.

Danger time.

The tents had all been pitched in a circle. I noticed that while Joe and I shared a tent, Samantha had her own. So did Tommy. His was placed next to hers, with Leila's on the other side.

Theo had placed his camera on top of Samantha's tent pole, cleverly disguised under a piece of canvas. I hadn't noticed him putting it up there in the dark, and I was pretty sure no one else had either.

The camera would provide a perfect view of the opening of Samantha's tent. If anyone tried anything funny, like they had on the boat, the camera would definitely catch them in the act.

I was pleased that I'd thought of the idea. Our job here was to keep Sam Chilton alive and well, but there was no way we could guard her twenty-four hours a day. All human beings need sleep, including us.

In fact, it didn't take fifteen minutes in his sleeping bag before Joe was snoring away. As for me, I tried to get to sleep, but it was impossible, what with my brother sawing wood like that.

I was just about to get out of my sleeping bag and give him a good shake when I saw a human figure standing at the opening of our tent.

I reached into my pocket, pulled out my flashlight, and shone it on the intruder.

It was Leila!

She put a hand over her eyes to shield her from the blinding light.

I switched it off and went over to her. "What's the matter?"

"I . . ." She glanced over at Joe, who was still snoring away. "Can we talk?"

"Uh, sure!" I said softly. Taking her arm, I led

her outside and let the tent flap fall closed behind me. "What's up?"

"I must talk to someone, and—I don't know why, but . . . well . . . I feel as though, somehow, I can trust you."

"Oh, you can!" I assured her. At the same time, I wondered why she'd picked me.

"You're not like the others, I can tell," she whispered, taking my hand in both of hers.

That's when I saw that her hands were all tattooed. Funny, I hadn't noticed it before.

She saw me staring at the dark red designs— swirling patterns that reminded me of spiderwebs. "It's henna," she explained. "A natural dye—it comes off after a few weeks. Egyptian women, especially here in the desert, use it for special occasions, to decorate themselves."

"What's the occasion?" I asked, curious.

"We are about to enter the presence of a great king," she said. She ran one finger of her right hand up and down the lines of the pattern on her left. "In honor of him, and of our glorious Egyptian history, I beautify myself."

She *was* beautiful—there was no doubt about it. At that moment, under the incredible blanket of stars, with her dark eyes flashing at me, I wanted to tell her how amazing she was—but all I said was, "Oh. I see."

What a dork!

I don't know what it is about me—every time I'm with a girl I like, I trip over my own feet. Just once, I'd love to say the perfect thing, you know? *Just once.*

Luckily, Leila seemed not to notice, or she didn't care. Something seemed to be weighing heavily on her mind, and for some reason she'd decided to share it with me.

All I had to do was keep quiet and listen.

"There is great danger—I can feel it," she said.

"What do you mean?" I wanted her to keep talking—but I could feel it too.

"Ms. Chilton—she is very foolish. She does not realize the evil she brings with her."

"Evil? You mean the mummy's curse?"

She snorted. "Mummy's curse? Don't be stupid."

I felt like a total airhead. Leila was studying for a master's degree, so she was obviously intelligent and well educated. But it was her attitude that made me feel so dumb. Like I should know without asking that there's no such thing as a mummy's curse.

Well, I *did* know—and I didn't. I mean, out there in the dark desert night, you could almost *feel* the danger closing in.

"The Golden Mummy and his treasure are cursed, all right," she said. "Cursed by *human greed*. Some people have no respect for history or culture—and if bad things happen to them, they will have only themselves to blame."

Uh-oh. Was she threatening somebody? Had I read Leila Abdul the wrong way?

I could feel a deep anger surging behind her eyes. Was she angry enough to hurt someone?

SUSPECT PROFILE

<u>Name:</u> Leila Abdul

<u>Hometown:</u> Cairo, Egypt

<u>Physical description:</u> Age 22, 5' 8", 125 lbs., dark hair, penetrating eyes, a real beauty.

<u>Occupation:</u> Graduate student, University of Cairo, studying for a master's degree in Egyptology; assistant to Dr. Mounir

<u>Hobby:</u> Not sure. Working on it.

<u>Background:</u> Grew up in a wealthy Cairo family of diplomats. Traveled and studied all over the world. Speaks seven languages, has always been the brightest student in class.

"Is that all you wanted to tell me?" I asked her.

She shook her head. "I saw someone . . . sneaking around Ms. Chilton's tent."

"You did? Who was it?"

"Theo."

"Ah."

What else could I say? I knew why Theo had been there—he'd been setting up the video surveillance Joe and I had asked for. But I couldn't tell that to Leila, could I?

"I . . . wouldn't be too worried about that," I said. "It probably has something to do with the video they're making."

She made a face. "You don't believe me! I was wrong about you—you're just like the others."

83

No! I'm not, I wanted to say.

But of course, I didn't.

"You will see," she said, "that the closer we get to the treasure, the more the curse of greed will come to haunt us all." She turned and walked away into the darkness, heading for her tent.

I stared after her until she disappeared behind her tent flap, then went back and lay down on my cot, thinking about all she'd said.

What had she really been trying to tell me? Who did she think was greedy? Who was dangerous?

My thoughts were suddenly interrupted by a scream from Samantha's tent.

"Oh, no!" Joe said, sitting up and rubbing his eyes. "Not again!"

He was already up and moving—Joe to the rescue. "If somebody's laid a hand on her, I'll—"

I followed him outside. Everyone was rushing toward Sam's tent. Then she appeared, lifting her tent flap and shouting, "It's gone! Somebody stole my belly bag!"

She didn't have to say what was inside the belly bag. Joe and I gave each other a quick look.

The map of the Golden Mummy's tomb was gone!

I went over to Theo and tapped him on the arm. "Did we get it all on tape?" I asked.

"I'll go see," he said, and went to retrieve the hidden camera.

Meanwhile, Tommy was ranting and raving about how he was going to find out who stole the bag and break their neck for them. He seemed to be yelling mostly at Mounir's group of thugs.

Leila, in turn, was glaring at Tommy. "Leave them alone!" she was saying. "You don't know it was them. Don't you dare assume it! It was probably one of *you* who did it—maybe even you yourself!"

Tommy and Leila started screaming at each other, and Dr. Mounir soon joined in on Leila's side. I could see Dr. Volsky trying to get a word in, but his voice wasn't loud enough to be heard.

In the meantime, Joe was trying to get the story of what happened from Samantha. I followed them both inside her tent.

"I guess I fell asleep," she was saying. "I was dreaming that my map—you know, the one I told you I always keep on me—was being stolen. And then I woke up, and my belly bag was gone!"

"I assume the map was inside?" I asked.

"Uh-huh. I always wore it under my shirt, so no one could take it."

"Were you wearing it while you slept?" Joe asked.

"No, that would have been really uncomfortable," she said. "I put the belly bag under my pillow instead."

"Bad move," Joe said. "But don't worry—we'll get it back for you. Somebody here's got it, and we're going to find it."

She smiled and stroked Joe's cheek. "Thank you," she said, giving him a kiss. "You're very sweet. Even sweeter than Tommy."

Now it was my turn to enjoy the sight of Joe acting geeky. His mouth kept opening and closing like a fish, but he couldn't think of a single thing to say.

Nice moves, bro, I thought. *Very smooth.*

Theo lifted the tent flap. He held the camera in his other hand. "We've got the thief on tape, red-handed," he said.

He sat down on the edge of Samantha's cot, and we all watched the monitor as someone sneaked into Samantha's tent, then, a couple of minutes later, crept back out.

Leila!

I couldn't believe it. She'd just now come to me to warn me about how greedy people were—and here she was, stealing other people's property!

Of course, it all made sense. If she didn't want greedy people to get their hands on the treasure, what better way to prevent it than by stealing the map of the tomb?

But wait . . .

"Could you run that tape back again?" I asked.

Theo did, and this time I saw that when she emerged, Leila's hands were empty. "Where's the belly bag?" I asked.

Theo shrugged. "Maybe under her robe?"

"Why don't we just ask her?" Joe suggested.

We went outside. Mounir's men had brought lanterns, and the whole encampment was lit with an eerie orange glow.

"Leila," I said. "Where's the belly bag?"

"What?" Her eyes widened in shock. "I didn't take it!"

"We have you on video," Theo said, holding up the camera.

"But I swear I didn't take it! I went into Ms. Chilton's tent, yes—but only to make sure she was all right!"

Nobody seemed more shocked than Dr. Mounir. "Leila, is this true?" he asked. "Did you steal from the young lady? I cannot believe it!"

"No! No, I didn't! The bag was still there when I left the tent."

"How would you know that," Sam challenged

her, "unless you'd looked under my pillow?"

Everyone's eyes were on Leila, who looked like she was about to panic.

"Search her tent," Tommy ordered, and three of Mounir's crew went into action, searching Leila's tent. A few minutes later, they came out again—empty-handed.

"Sam," Tommy said, "she's still got it on her. Search her."

Sam seemed to hesitate. "Is . . . is that all right?" she asked Leila. "Can I?"

Leila looked around, at all the men surrounding her. "In private," she said. The two women went into Samantha's tent, then came out again.

"She's clean," Sam said. "Obviously, she's telling the truth."

"It's her," Theo insisted. "There's no denying the tape. She must have stashed it somewhere."

"Theo," I said, getting an idea, "maybe someone else *also* went into Samantha's tent. Try running the tape farther forward!"

He held up the camera, and everyone crowded around to try and get a glimpse of the monitor. We saw Leila emerge from the tent, empty-handed. Then we saw five minutes of the tent at night—no one going in or out.

"That's enough of this," Tommy said. "It's her, all right. She must have hidden the belly bag somewhere. Come on, let's tear this whole place apart!"

"Wait!" I said. "Be patient. The tape's not over yet."

"How long do you expect us to stand here and—"

Just then, another figure appeared on the monitor: One of Mounir's camel drivers, the one with the eye patch. He looked around to make sure no one was watching him, then ducked inside Samantha's tent—and reemerged with the belly bag in his hands.

Everyone gasped and looked around, but the camel driver on the tape was nowhere to be found.

"He's got to be around here somewhere," Tommy said. "Check the camels, and see if they're all still here. If he took off, we can still catch up to him by following the camel's tracks."

All the camels were still in camp. If the driver had run away, he'd gone on foot—a suicidal move, considering civilization was a full day's camel ride away, and he had no camel.

"Find him!" Dr. Mounir ordered, and his men scattered, carrying their lanterns high.

Soon enough, there was a shout from one of them. We followed the sound of his voice to a nearby gully. He stood at the bottom, his lantern held up high, so that we could see his find.

It was the camel driver who'd been caught on video. And there was no doubt about it. . . .

He was stone cold dead.

8.
The Shadow of Death

There's something about a dead body that gives you the creeps. Almost always, it's lying in a position that no living person would ever be in.

The guy with the eye patch looked like he was lying down, doubled over. When we got closer we could see that the back of his head had a huge bump on it where he'd been hit with something big.

His hand, frozen in death, was still clutching Sam's belly bag.

For a moment nobody moved—I guess none of us wanted to touch the body. Then Tommy broke out of it. He grabbed the bag from the dead man's hand and looked inside. "It's empty."

Whoever killed the camel driver now had the

map of the Golden Mummy's tomb. We had no idea who the murderer could be, and we were in the middle of a vast desert.

We were in trouble.

Mounir's four remaining guides and drivers took away their dead comrade while Tommy started yelling. "*Now* what are we supposed to do?" he asked over and over again, without waiting for an answer. "We're totally finished!"

"Shut up, Tommy!" Sam yelled at him. "Just zip it, okay? We're going ahead with this no matter what, okay?"

"Dr. Mounir is behind all this!" Volsky yelled, pointing his finger at him.

"Me? It is you, Volsky! You have been trying to sabotage my career for years. You'll stop at nothing, I see—not even murder!"

Leila stood by, listening to them all shouting at one another, her eyes and expression hidden by her scarf. What was she thinking?

Theo had grabbed his camera. He, Nels, and Jurgen were recording the whole crazy scene for reality TV. Their show was going on, no doubt.

Tommy was now cursing and threatening anyone who would listen—mostly the film crew and poor Ahmed, who was trying his best to sympathize with everyone.

"You!" Sam suddenly shouted, pointing to me and Frank. "You two!"

She marched toward us, backing us up until we were all standing in front of her tent, out of earshot of the rest of the party. "You said you were reporters, but I know you're lying," she said, fuming with anger.

"Us? Lying?" I said, trying to sound innocent. "What do you mean?"

"Yeah, what makes you say that?" Frank asked.

"For one thing, you never take any notes. You don't even carry pens and pads!"

Oops. I guess we'd kind of overlooked that part.

Sam wasn't done with us. "Who are you, *really*? And what are you doing here? Don't lie to me—I can see right through you."

I looked at Frank, signaling him to say something. After all, he's supposed to be the brainy one.

He sighed, and his shoulders sank. "Guilty as charged," he admitted.

I rolled my eyes in disbelief. *What was he doing?*

"Aha!" Sam said, pointing her finger at us. "I knew it!"

Frank looked around. "Could we, um, go inside the tent and talk about this?"

Sam frowned, but she held open the tent flap for us to go inside.

93

"We were sent here to *protect* you," Frank continued once we were inside.

Sam's mouth fell open. "Tommy said my mom sent you here to spy on us. Is that true?"

"Not exactly," Frank said, not mentioning ATAC. "Your mom was worried about you, all right, but that isn't how we came to be here. Samantha, as we told you earlier, there is a threat to your life."

Sam blinked, startled. "But who would want to hurt me? Everybody *loves* me!"

I couldn't help thinking that Sam, for all her fine qualities—including her fantastic looks—just wasn't all that bright.

"Lots of people would love to get their hands on the Golden Mummy's treasure," Frank pointed out. "If someone knew that Roger Corson gave you the map . . ."

"But . . . but *nobody* knew I had the map," Sam said. "Nobody except me, my mom, and Tommy, and . . . you two guys!"

Her eyes widened in sudden fear.

"Don't worry," I said. "It wasn't us. Like Frank said, we're here to protect you. And we didn't tell anyone about it either."

"But somebody clearly figured it out," Frank added. "Samantha, you say you told Tommy?"

"I don't know why I should trust you two," Sam said, "after the way you've lied to me already."

"We *had* to lie," I protested. "You would never have let us come along with you if we'd told you the truth!"

"I guess you're right about that," Sam admitted. "Say, who sent you anyway? My mother?"

Frank and I looked at one another.

"I knew it!" Sam said, and we didn't argue with her.

"Besides," Frank said, "you *have* to trust us. We're the only ones here with no reason to try and cheat you out of finding the treasure."

"Not to mention the fame that comes with it," I added.

"So . . . I can't even trust my *Poopsie*?" Sam's voice was small and soft, like the voice of a wounded child.

"*Especially* not him," I said. "Sam, you've only known the guy, what, three weeks? He could easily be interested in you just for your family's money."

"Not to mention the chance to get at the mummy's treasure," Frank said.

Sam blinked back tears. She seemed really shaken up. I could tell that our words had gotten to her. "I . . . I just can't believe he would steal from me. Let alone kill somebody."

"Well, we don't know that he did," Frank said. "But from here on in, we'd better be careful—that is, if you still want to keep going."

Sam blinked in surprise. I could tell she hadn't even considered the possibility of turning back. "Why wouldn't I?" she said. "I mean, I remember enough about the map to get us to the Valley of the Serpents and find the tomb entrance."

"And once we're inside the tomb?" Frank asked.

Sam frowned. "Well, I guess at that point we'll have to take our chances and trust our luck. But no *way* am I going to turn back and let whoever stole my map steal everything!"

There were shouts from the gully where the body had been discovered. Men were yelling, and I heard Leila shouting back at them.

Frank looked worried. "I'd better go see if she's all right," he said, and left.

Sam and I were alone together, for the first time. She was crying softly, wiping the tears from her eyes. I wanted to take her in my arms and kiss her, but I wasn't sure she felt the same about me. So I chickened out.

I pulled a clean hanky out of my pocket and offered it to her. She took it and dried her face off. "Thanks," she said, letting out a little half laugh, half sob.

"You okay?" I asked.

"I guess."

"You know, you could just give up, and we could all go home and forget the whole thing."

"Are you suggesting I do that?" she asked.

"It would be safer for you. My job is to keep you safe, remember."

"But if you were me?"

I smiled. "If I were you? I'd keep going, just to stick it to whoever killed my ex-boyfriend and that thieving camel driver."

Now she was smiling. Her eyes glistened up at me gratefully. "See?" she said. "Thank you for understanding."

She reached over and kissed me on the cheek.

I felt my knees get suddenly weak, but I steeled myself. I had to keep my distance, even if I was passing up the dating opportunity of a lifetime. I had a job to do.

"I'd . . . better go see how Frank is doing," I said, backing away from her slowly.

As I reached the tent flap, I picked up a heavy flashlight and tossed it gently to her. "If anyone comes in, just bop them over the head with that and yell for help. I'll come running."

"Thanks, Joe," she said, giving me a warm smile. "I won't forget this."

"Me neither," I said, lifting the tent flap and going outside.

OOOF!!

No sooner had I let the flap drop than a ton of bricks rammed into my side and knocked me to the ground.

Next thing I knew, Tommy was pummeling my gut with both of his humongous fists.

"Lay off my girlfriend, you scum!" he grunted, socking me over and over again.

I wanted to explain things to him, but it's not easy when you've had the breath knocked out of you. Man, this guy had fists of steel. His punches *hurt*!

I had no choice but to deliver a hard-driving kung fu combination to his solar plexus. It sent him reeling ten feet backward.

Yeah, I've still got it.

As for me, well, everything hurt. I limped over to where Tommy lay, groaning, near a heap of camel dung.

"I wish you'd have let me explain," I said. "Sam and I were just talking, okay? No need to get so twisted up about it. And what are you *really* upset about, anyway? Losing your girl? Or losing her treasure map?"

"I'll get you for this," Tommy muttered. Drool

dribbled out the side of his mouth as he lay there on the ground. "When you least expect it, I'll pay you back, big-time."

I brushed the dust off my hands, and it sprinkled down onto his face. "Don't make me humiliate you again—*Poopsie*," I said, leaving him there to recover his senses.

It's *good* to know kung fu.

The next morning, the sun rose big and blood red over the desert. In a matter of fifteen minutes, the temperature went from freezing cold to unbearably hot.

Dr. Mounir sent the body of the dead camel driver back to Ras Khalifa, along with another driver and two of our camels. Then the rest of us broke camp and headed farther west.

Frank and I dropped back to the rear of our little camel caravan, so that we could talk freely and compare notes. "Do you think that camel driver stole the map on his own?" I asked.

"No. He was working for Mounir, remember?"

"So are all of them," I pointed out. "Including Leila."

Frank stiffened. "Leila's no pushover. She thinks for herself."

"How does she feel about Mounir?"

"She doesn't think much of his curse theories," he said. "I don't think she trusts him much either."

"Smart girl. So if the dead guy stole the map for someone else, who do you think it was?"

"Well, we know the guy was working for Dr. Mounir. But that doesn't mean he stole it for him. Anybody on the expedition could have paid him to do it."

"Why not steal it themselves?" I asked.

"Well, if they tried and got caught, it would be the end of everything for them. Remember, they took the trouble last time to disguise the thief as a mummy. If they sent someone else to do it, and *that* person got caught, they could deny hiring him. No need for a disguise."

"Right," I said. "And whoever did hire that guy took the map from him, and then killed him so he couldn't reveal the truth."

"Totally. So, other than Mounir, who could it be?"

"I nominate Tommy," I said. "He's the only one here that Sam told about the map."

"I hate to say it, bro, but Sam Chilton has . . . how shall I say, a big mouth? It's totally possible she let it slip to Dr. Mounir or Dr. Volsky, or even to one of the video guys."

"Maybe," I said. "But Tommy's definitely dangerous, and I'll bet you he was only interested in Sam to get near her treasure map."

I proceeded to tell Frank about getting jumped by Tommy Testosterone.

"If Tommy had killed that guy, he'd have the map," Frank said. "And he wouldn't have been so angry."

"True," I said, "although he might have just been angry about me flirting with Sam."

"*Were* you flirting with Sam?" he asked.

"Just a little."

He gave me a look.

"What, am I not allowed a moment of happiness?"

"Why, Joe, I thought fighting crime gave you happiness."

"Ha-ha. So, speaking of crime, who else could it be?"

"Could be Dr. Volsky," Frank said. "He's been awfully quiet. And don't forget our chef."

"The Happy Hippie?"

"He got hired at the last minute—by cheating, remember—and no one has checked him out at all. I say he bears watching."

"Agreed. Anyone else?"

Frank shrugged. "Could be anyone except you or me. Whoever has the map is holding all the cards. But he or she won't show his or her hand until we get to the tomb."

"Let's hope not," I said. "One dead body is more than enough."

When it got too hot to go any farther, we stopped for lunch. The drivers pitched a big dinner tent—really, just a roof without walls—and Ahmed went to work preparing our meal.

It was close to four in the afternoon by the time we ate. Soon the sun would be low enough in the sky for us to continue onward into the evening.

Everyone sat down in a circle. It was hot, and we were moving slowly. Dr. Mounir slapped at the back of his neck before lowering his bulk to the ground.

"Ouch!" he said.

"What's the matter?" Leila asked.

"Something just stung me," he said. "A bee, I think."

Ahmed put out bowls of grapes and dates, nuts and figs. Then he served a lamb stew, giving Dr. Mounir his bowl first, as a sign of respect for his high position in government.

Dr. Mounir tasted the stew as Ahmed continued to give out the steaming bowls. "Ahhh! Delicious!" he said, savoring it. "My highest compliments to the che . . . urghlhgh . . ."

102

Suddenly he was choking, wheezing, his eyes bulging out. Leila grabbed the steaming bowl of stew from his hands as Tommy tried slapping Mounir on the back.

"Are you okay?" he asked. Mounir was quickly turning blue. He slumped in Tommy's arms, and not even the former Mr. Universe could hold up the bulky Egyptian official.

Dr. Mounir was a dead weight—with the emphasis on *dead*.

9.
The Mark of Poison

The second Dr. Mounir practically fell face-first into his bowl of lamb stew, his entire crew of shady camel drivers whipped out their long, curved knives and started yelling like they were going to slit all of our throats.

All of us gasped at once—except for Leila, who was together enough to take Mounir's pulse to make sure he was really dead.

He was.

His men were still yelling in Arabic for all they were worth. No one was sure what they were going to do until they all turned at once toward Ahmed, the Happy Hippie, whose lamb stew had presumably brought the great Dr. Mounir down.

One of the thugs grabbed Ahmed and dragged him to the table. "Eat!" he commanded.

Ahmed took Dr. Mounir's bowl of stew and, with just a little hesitation—there were three knives at his throat, after all—he ate a mouthful.

"Mmmm!" he said, nodding and smacking his lips. "Good!"

He ate another mouthful, then another—so quickly that half of it spilled all over his white robe.

But he didn't die. He didn't even look sick. Mounir's thugs, seeing that the stew wasn't poisoned after all, let him go, and Ahmed collapsed to the ground, shaking all over—no longer the Happy Hippie, but definitely grateful to be alive.

Mounir's crew of thugs, meanwhile, resumed yelling and waving their knives. Their eyes were now white with horror, and I could guess the reason why. If Mounir's food wasn't poisoned, something else must have killed him.

He had been a great believer in the mummy's curse, and apparently, so were his men. They ran, screaming, from the tent.

By the time the rest of us recovered enough from our shock to get up and follow them, our guides and porters were already riding off to the east with half of our remaining camels and most of our supplies—including the shortwave radio set we'd brought along so that we could stay in touch with the rest of the world.

Now we were truly, totally alone out here, with three camels, some picks and shovels, enough food for maybe five days, a whole lot of heavy video equipment, and a big, fat, dead body.

And night was coming on fast.

Joe and I kneeled over Dr. Mounir, examining the body, while Leila went to get some tent nylon to serve as a shroud.

"He complained of a bee sting just before he sat down to eat," I reminded Joe. "And he slapped at the back of his neck."

Joe turned Mounir's head to the side. There, just behind his right ear, was a small, red puncture wound. "I guess he was allergic to bees," he said.

"I don't think so," said Dr. Volsky, who had come up behind us. "There are no bees this far into the desert. No plants, no flowers—therefore no bees."

"Then what stung him?" Joe asked.

"I think," said Dr. Volsky, examining the wound on Mounir's neck, "that Dr. Mounir was felled by a poison dart."

"A poison dart!" Joe said. "What kind of poison could knock a guy that size flat so quickly, and with so small a dose?"

"That," said Dr. Volsky, "is no mystery at all. Have you never heard of curare?"

"Curare? Yeah, that's a South American plant," I said.

"I believe that is what killed Dr. Mounir," Volsky said. "Of course, we'll never know now. Curare leaves no trace in the body, and the dart—well, whoever shot it would have picked it up while the rest of us were running around, panicked."

It was as good an explanation as any. I liked it a whole lot better than the mummy's curse theory. You can catch a criminal who's still alive. A four-thousand-year-old bag of bones, on the other hand, could be a whole lot tougher.

We buried Dr. Mounir in a temporary grave. At some point, the government would want to dig him up and have a big funeral for him in the city where he'd lived and become famous. For now, we marked his grave with a broken ax handle and a piece of white cloth to serve as a flag and a marker.

Leila said some prayers over the grave, and then we got back to business, setting up our tents for the night. There were fewer tents now—and fewer of us to sleep in them.

"Tomorrow morning, we must head back to Ras Khalifa," Leila said as we worked.

"Head back?" Tommy repeated. "No way! No possible way!"

"Perhaps she is right," Dr. Volsky said. "Without Dr. Mounir . . ."

"I thought you two couldn't stand each other," Tommy said. "Since when is Mounir the be-all and end-all?"

"I'm in charge of this expedition now that Dr. Mounir is dead," said Leila. "As his assistant, I am the highest-ranking official of the Egyptian government with this expedition. And I say we go back in the morning."

Samantha stepped forward, getting right in Leila's face. "Oh, yeah?" she said, her hands on her hips. "Well, you can go back tomorrow if you want. But the rest of us are going on to the tomb, and we're taking the camels and the supplies with us."

"But—" Leila tried to protest, but Tommy stepped into the argument, pointing his finger right in her face.

"Listen, sweetheart," he said, "you're nothing but a graduate student, okay? And this—this is Sam Chilton, okay? Her mom is *Lady* Chilton? Her dad was *Lord* Chilton? They can buy and sell your entire university any day of the week. So if she says we're going to the tomb, we're going to the tomb."

"That would be illegal," said Leila, holding her

ground. "When you return to Ras Khalifa, you will be arrested by the police."

"I don't think so," Sam said, slipping one arm through Tommy's. "I think if we offer the Egyptian government a piece of our hot new reality TV series—*The Mummy's Tomb, Revealed*—they'll go easy on us. Don't you think so, Theo?"

"Definitely," said Theo, who was recording the whole scene with a handheld camera. "Nels?"

"No doubt," said Nels, his arms folded across his chest.

"I think so too," said Jurgen, who was holding up the boom mike to capture every word.

"Dr. Volsky?" Leila pleaded. "Surely you can see that it would be madness to continue."

"Er, yes," he agreed in a soft voice, "but on the other hand, think of the priceless artifacts we might uncover. . . ."

Leila stared right through him. "You are a fool, for all your scientific knowledge," she declared. Then she looked at Frank and me. "Well?"

I was about to tell her I agreed with her, and that the sensible thing to do would be to turn back until a new expedition could be mounted—one with police protection from whoever, or whatever, was cursing this one. But Joe spoke up first.

"If Sam's going on, then so are we," he said.

I wanted to argue with him, to stand up for Leila. But I knew he was right.

Our job was to protect Samantha Chilton. If she was going on with this madness, we had to come along for the ride—because whether or not the mummy's curse was real, there was definitely someone murderous on the loose. Someone—or *something*—who might strike again at any moment.

Leila curled her hands into fists and let out a frustrated growl. Then she stomped off to her tent and let the flap fall behind her.

I wanted to go after her, to make sure she was all right. I knew she had to be pretty upset after watching her boss die, and being accused of stealing Samantha's map.

But I also knew that my job was not to make sure Leila was okay. It was to protect Samantha Chilton.

So when Joe suggested we sleep right in front of Sam's tent, out under the stars—just in case anybody got any more deadly ideas—I agreed, and we went to get our sleeping bags.

Leila would have to fend for herself, at least for tonight.

Our sleeping bags were all laid out for us, much to our surprise. I guessed we had Ahmed to thank, since I couldn't picture anyone else taking the trouble.

Our air pillows were in place, right where we'd want to lay our heads. I picked mine up, ready to grab the sleeping bag, too . . . and found about a dozen scorpions, their deadly stingers held high and ready to strike.

111

10.
The Sting of Betrayal

If you've never been scared within an inch of your life, let me describe it for you. Your heart goes into instant overdrive. Your ears start ringing. Your breath comes in short gasps, and you want to run, but your legs won't move because your knees have turned to rubber.

Now, to be fair, Frank and I were only scared for a split second. Once we'd backed away to a safe distance, we calmed right down—but if we'd gone to sleep as usual that night, we'd have been stung at least ten times apiece by the time we knew what was happening.

We'd have been dead, that's what. Dead as Roger Corson. Dead as Dr. Mounir and the camel driver who'd stolen Sam's treasure map.

"Okay," I said, forcing myself to breathe normally, "now, who do we think would do a nasty thing like this?"

"Let's see," Frank said, "Dr. Mounir and his camel drivers are off the hook; the last of them left before we pitched camp for the night. That leaves Samantha, Tommy, Dr. Volsky, Theo, Nels, Jurgen, Ahmed . . ."

"And your pretty friend Leila," I added. "Don't forget her."

"She wouldn't do something like this," Frank said. "Did you see how pale she looked when Dr. Mounir died? She was totally shocked."

"Not too shocked to take his pulse," I said. "You'd better watch it, bro. Don't let your latest crush get in the way of your usual good judgment."

"I'm telling you, she's okay."

"Whatever, dude. But just remember we've got a killer on the loose."

We broke camp before first light and were on our way again by sunrise. We had decided not to say anything about the scorpions, to see if somebody looked shocked to see us alive. Nobody gave it away, though somebody had a great "poker face."

Loading up the camels was tough. None of us had any experience with them, except for Ahmed and Dr. Volsky, who'd been on a few expeditions in his time. The camels didn't seem to want to be loaded down. They kept bucking, kicking, and spitting.

Nobody said much as we rode westward toward a distant wall of red sandstone cliffs. Everyone was looking at everyone else with suspicion; even Tommy and Sam exchanged a few wary looks. We were coming closer, and we could all feel the excitement—and the danger.

Sam had told Frank and me that she could get us as far as the tomb entrance from her memory of the map.

Only the killer knew where to go once we were inside. Whoever had the map was just waiting until we got there to make his move.

I wondered what that move would be. I could hardly wait to find out.

Just before noon, we rounded the end of a ridge and found ourselves in the long-hidden Valley of the Serpents. Cliffs rose up on both sides of us, as high and as red as the Grand Canyon's walls. It was an amazing sight, and everyone rode silently, feeling the presence of ancient ghosts hovering over us.

We stopped before a pile of rubble that lay in front of the cliff. "This is the spot," Sam said, dismounting.

"You sure, baby?" Tommy asked, looking doubtful. "Seems like just a pile of rocks to me."

"Duh, that's the whole idea," Sam said, rolling her eyes. "Roger put the rocks there to disguise the entrance so nobody would find it."

She directed the video crew to set up for recording. Meanwhile, Ahmed, Volsky, Tommy, Leila, Frank, and I unloaded our remaining camels and set up our tents.

When Theo, Nels, and Jurgen were ready, we formed a sort of human conveyor belt and began removing the rocks from the tomb entrance. After about five minutes, it was clear that this exercise was going to take a long time if everybody wasn't helping. So everyone, from the video crew to Sam Chilton herself, had to get their hands dirty.

Finally, just as we were about to call it quits for the day, Tommy let out a whoop. "Paydirt!"

Everyone rushed over to where he was standing. There was a little dark hole in the giant mound of rubble, and a cool breeze blew from below it. It stank of age, and decay, and who knew what else.

Ten minutes later we had cleared the entrance

enough for one person at a time to pass through. Sam went in first, since she was the one who'd organized and paid for this whole expedition. Tommy was about to step through next, but I got in there before him.

"Hey!" he complained.

"Let him come in first, Tommy," Sam ordered.

She understood why I'd stepped in Tommy's way. I was her first line of protection. Nobody could be trusted now that we'd found the tomb— nobody except me and Frank, that is.

Next, the video equipment was handed through. Nels, Theo, and Jurgen came in through the entrance, then Tommy, Frank, Volsky, and Leila.

Ahmed called in to us through the gap in the rubble. "I shall stay out here and guard our equipment and the camels!" he said.

"You get yourself in here, Mr. Happy Hippie," Tommy said, scowling. Turning to Sam, he said, "I can just see him burying us all alive in here."

"Why would he do that?" Sam asked. "Even if he's the one who stole my map, if he sealed the entrance to the tomb, he'd never get the treasure."

Tommy blinked several times. "Oh. Yeah, I guess you're right," he said. "Okay, Ahmed," he called. "You can stay."

The light on the video camera lit our way down the passage from the entrance. The main hallway turned sharply to the right, heading downward.

Here and there, smaller passages led left and right. The cool breeze was still blowing at us from up ahead.

"I think the map had us turning off the main passage to the right," Sam said, "but I can't really remember how far in it was. . . ."

We were lost without the map; that was the simple truth. We were going to have to wander around in here until we stumbled on the burial chamber by accident and sheer luck.

"We should leave markers where we've been, so we won't keep going around in circles," Frank suggested, using his small pocketknife to tear a piece of cloth off the bottom of his shirt.

It was a good idea. From then on, every time we turned, we left a scrap of cloth, weighted down with a pebble, to mark our way. We wandered into several dead ends and marked them with two pieces of cloth instead of just one. As we went, Frank tried to draw his own map on a pocket notepad.

I don't know whether I was more scared of the mummy's curse at this point or of the living people I was surrounded by. At least one of them was a killer who would surely commit murder again to get at the mummy's treasure.

But which one?

Finally, Sam said, "I think we've done enough for today. I'm starving and dead tired. Let's mark this spot, and we'll start from here tomorrow morning."

Nels had been carrying an unlit oil lamp with him, just in case the camera's light ran out of power. He now placed the lantern on the floor at a three-way junction of passages. He took out a match, struck it on the stone wall, lit the lantern, then threw the match to the ground.

It landed at the side of the wall, in a small shallow trench that I hadn't noticed until that moment. It ran along the length of the stone wall—and was apparently filled with some sort of oil.

Within seconds it was filled with flames.

The fire raced along the side of the wall, ahead of us, and down the corridor, until it disappeared around another corner. We followed.

The flames led us to a musty staircase leading downward. The line of flame zigzagged down the steps to another, deeper level of the tomb.

The steps were blocked by gigantic spiderwebs— with gigantic spiders still in them. Sam shrieked in disgust until Tommy, Jurgen, and Theo took care of the spiders. I swear, they were the size of silver dollars.

We followed the line of flame around several more corners, until it came to a sudden end at a pile of rocks that totally blocked the passageway.

It looked a lot like the pile outside the tomb entrance, except that this pile was covered with centuries of dust. It looked like no one had disturbed it since it was first put in place.

"It must be the burial chamber of the Golden Mummy!" Dr. Volsky said excitedly. "What an incredible stroke of luck!"

"Yes," Leila said. "It's as if someone, or something, was leading us right to this spot . . . as if it wanted us to find whatever lies behind these stones. . . ."

A shiver went right up my spine.

Leila was right—someone must have been expecting us.

And that couldn't be good.

I got the strong feeling that we were heading straight into an ancient, deadly trap.

FRANK

11.
The Serpent's Tooth

It was an awesome moment—you could see it in the eyes of every one of us, reflected by the light of the line of fire that had led us here without a map.

If it hadn't been for that lucky break, we might have been inside this tomb for weeks, looking in vain for the burial chamber. Now all we had to do was dig.

"We're going to need the pickaxes and sledgehammers," Tommy said.

"You folks go on back," Theo said. "Nels, Jurgen, and I will set up the shoot for tomorrow—then we can leave the heavy equipment in place and just bring fresh batteries when we come back."

"I'm not leaving this spot until everyone else

does," Tommy said, looking around at the rest of us. "One of you is a killer, and I'm not leaving Sam at a killer's mercy."

"Who says you're not the killer yourself?" Leila told Tommy. "What exactly are your qualifications for this expedition, anyway?"

"Maybe we'd all better help the video guys set up, and then go back outside together," I suggested, before a fight got started.

"Right," Joe agreed, backing me up. "We can eat supper, sleep, and come back tomorrow—together. That way, nobody can pull any funny business."

Everyone looked at everybody else.

"Good idea," Sam finally said, and that settled it.

In spite of the fact that she no longer had the map, she still seemed to be the boss. I guess it was just the sheer force of her personality.

We retraced our steps. Since the guiding fire had begun to burn out, we marked our way by our usual method, with strips of cloth and pebbles.

We made it back to the tomb entrance and emerged into the glare of the setting sun. Ahmed had been cooking; we could tell from the delicious smells coming from the fire pit he'd made.

"Couscous tonight!" Ahmed said cheerfully. "How was the search?"

"We found the burial chamber!" Tommy said, smiling.

Ahmed did not seem happy to hear it. "Already?" he said, looking distinctly worried. "Then, alas, the curse will soon be unleashed."

"Hey, I thought you were the *happy* hippie," Samantha said. "Cheer up! It means we can find the treasure and get out of here fast."

"Not fast enough," Ahmed muttered, dishing out portions of food. "Evil is in the air tonight. Ancient evil . . ."

I was beginning to get the chills myself—not that I'm inclined to believe in mummies coming back to life. But Ahmed was right about evil being in the air. All of us could feel it.

We all said good night and went to our tents, but we all knew nobody was going to sleep that night. Everyone was going to be watching everyone else—and listening with one cocked ear for the sounds of the dead arising.

Joe and I lay in our sleeping bags fully dressed, just in case. We kept still, listening for the sounds of someone moving.

And soon, we heard it. Footfalls, coming closer . . .

Our tent flap rose—and there was Tommy's chiseled face, staring in at us.

Well, at least it wasn't a mummy.

Joe and I both sat up. "What are you doing here?" Joe asked him.

"Just checking on everybody," Tommy said.

"Oh," I said.

"So, good night then." He let down the flap and proceeded on his rounds.

"It's good somebody's checking," Joe said.

"Yeah," I replied, "but that somebody should be us."

"Right," he said. "Soon as things settle down again."

We waited for Tommy to finish and hit the sack. Then we waited some more.

"Are those more footsteps?" Joe whispered.

"Not sure. I think so, but they're softer than Tommy's."

"That could mean it's somebody smaller."

"Or that somebody's trying to sneak around."

We both sat up. "I'll check the tents on the right," I said. "You get the ones on the left."

"Right," answered Joe.

"No, left."

"Will you cut that out?" Joe said. He was already crawling out of his sleeping bag.

"Just want you to get it right."

"Right, so I go left."

"Right."

"Cut it out!"

The pitter-patter of sneaky footsteps had faded by then. By the light of the rising, nearly full moon, we could see the big tent of the video crew, our double tent, and the five single tents.

I peered into the tent just to the right of ours. Sam was sleeping peacefully. The next one was Tommy's.

"What are you doin'?" he asked, sitting up as I peered in.

"Just checking," I said.

"I already did."

"I know. Just checking again."

"Oh. Okay."

I let the flap down and continued on.

What a dunce that Tommy was! He seemed way too stupid to be the master thief and killer among us—but then again, he could have just been really good at *playing* dumb.

I lifted the flap of the next tent. Leila's.

She was lying on her side. Her eyes were closed, and her henna-tattooed hands rested under her cheek.

She was so beautiful, with the moon beaming down on her. . . .

Something was moving on the floor. Moving quickly, and slithering toward Leila's peaceful, beautiful face.

A snake!

A cold shiver went down my spine as it rose to strike, baring its fangs. . . .

12.

The Missing Man

I'd just finished peeking in on Dr. Volsky and Ahmed, both of whom seemed to be sleeping, when I heard Leila's scream. I got to her tent just in time to see Frank pick up a shovel and bring its sharp edge down hard. Over and over and over again.

Then I saw what it was: a snake! A big one, and poisonous, too, judging by the triangular shape of its head—which Frank had separated from its body, and not a moment too soon.

Both parts of the snake were less than two feet from Leila's sleeping bag—the end where her head had been before she scrambled out of bed and to her feet.

She was standing now, shuddering and sobbing, staring at the corpse of the animal that had almost killed her—would have, if not for Frank. She reached out and touched his arm, then came forward and kissed him on the cheek. "Thank you," she whispered. "Thank you for saving my life."

In the dim light, I couldn't see Frank blushing, but I knew he was. That's just Frank.

Other members of our party came over now, to see what all the fuss was about. I told them to back away, so Frank and Leila could get out of the tent. Then I told them all what had happened.

"Too bad we didn't get it on camera," Theo quipped. "It would have made a great scene for the TV show."

"Hey, man," Frank said angrily, "this is not some studio set. Somebody tried to kill Leila, okay? Probably the same person who's already killed two of us."

"*If* it was a person," Theo said, widening his eyes.

Frank shook his head. "Come on, Theo. What does it take before you start to take the danger seriously?"

"Who says the mummy's curse isn't real?" Theo asked.

"How else can you explain all the weird things that have happened?" Nels agreed.

"How do we even know that the snake was put there on purpose?" Sam asked. "It could have just, you know, wandered in there on its own, trying to keep warm."

"That snake did *not* just wander in there," Ahmed said, peeking inside the tent.

"Oh, yeah?" Sam said. "What do you know about it?"

"I know this desert," Ahmed replied. "I have lived here all my life, and I can tell you that that snake was not born in this desert, nor even in Egypt."

Suddenly there was a chill in the air. It grew colder in an instant, as if the dead were running their bony fingers across the backs of our necks.

"The mummy's curse," Jurgen echoed.

As if it needed saying.

I could feel my heart thumping crazily in my chest—and I'm sure I was the least scared of anybody there.

Anybody but Sam, that is. Nothing seemed to faze her. I'm not sure whether she was just born without the capacity for fear, or whether she was just too dumb to realize when she was in danger.

Either way, she wasn't scared now. "If that snake was put there on purpose, it wasn't by any mummy. It was by *one of you!*"

"Or *you*," Leila said, looking straight at Sam.

"That's ridiculous," Sam said. "Why would I try to mess up my own expedition?"

"Why, indeed?" said Leila.

The two women stood stock-still, looking daggers at each other. I thought they were about to go at it tooth and nail.

"Hey," I said, suddenly realizing there were too few people in our little group. "Where's Tommy?"

Everyone looked at everyone else, then all around.

Tommy wasn't there.

"Tommy!" Sam yelled. "Where are you?"

"Over here!" Tommy yelled back from the darkness that hid the entrance to the tomb. He tramped toward us, his face red with anger.

"Where have you been?" Sam asked, annoyed. "Do you know what just happened?"

"Somebody tried to kill Leila," Frank said.

"Oh, yeah?" Tommy said. "Well then, I know who it was."

"You do?" Sam asked.

"Yeah—Dr. Volsky."

Everyone looked around.

Volsky?

He wasn't there. He wasn't anywhere. . . .

Dr. Volsky had disappeared.

"The mummy must have got him!" Ahmed said, the whites of his eyes glowing in the light of the fire.

"Seriously, where could he have gone?" Sam asked.

Tommy's scowl grew even darker. "Figure it out," he said, turning his gaze back toward the entrance to the tomb.

SUSPECT PROFILE

<u>Name:</u> Dr. Igor Volsky

<u>Hometown:</u> Moscow, Russia

<u>Physical description:</u> 47 years old, 5' 6", 135 lbs., balding, thick glasses, goatee, speaks softly most of the time.

<u>Occupation:</u> World-famous expert on ancient Egypt, including tombs, pyramids, and mummies. Rival of Dr. Mounir—oops, better make that ex-rival

<u>Hobby:</u> Correcting mistakes in encyclopedias and textbooks.

<u>Background</u>: Grew up in Russia, educated in Paris, became famous when he decoded the Mysteries of the Monkey God, an ancient Egyptian text that led the way to finding the legendary Valley of the Princes, where many tombs and treasures were later dug up.

<u>Suspicious behavior</u>: Disappearing into the tomb alone while everyone else was distracted by Leila and the snake—or did the resulting commotion wake everyone up and alert them to his absence just by a stroke of luck?

<u>Suspected of</u>: Being behind the theft of the map, the deaths of the camel driver and Dr. Mounir, and attempts on the lives of the Hardys and Leila.

<u>Possible motive</u>: Getting the Golden Mummy's treasure for himself.

We got our flashlights together and raced into the tomb as a group. Even Ahmed came along this time, afraid to be left alone outside in the dark, in case the mummy showed up looking for more victims.

We got lost almost immediately. The fire in the little ditch by the side of the wall that had first led us to the burial chamber had long since gone out. And the shreds of cloth we'd dropped to mark our way had all been removed by Dr. Volsky.

At least, I *hoped* it was by Dr. Volsky. I mean, I don't normally believe in ghosts or mummies or anything like that. But right then, I could seriously imagine a real mummy appearing around the next corner of the passageway.

We wandered around, getting more and more lost. I sure hoped we could find our way out of this maze when we were done looking for Dr. Volsky.

"I think it was this way," Theo said, as we came to a junction. "To the left here, yes."

"No, it was farther on that we made the left," Tommy argued.

Everyone started arguing which way to go. Finally, Leila yelled, "Be quiet, all of you! Just *listen*."

It was good advice. The stone walls of the tomb made every sound echo. Once everyone had gone silent, and our own echoes stopped, we could hear something else—something soft and distant, but distinct.

The scraping of stone on stone. Like . . .

Like the cover of a sarcophagus being pushed open!

I could just picture Volsky in the burial chamber, that little pipsqueak, struggling to push the stone cover off the mummy's elaborate coffin. He must have already cleared the entrance to the burial chamber!

How big a head start had he gotten? He'd been in his sleeping bag when I checked on his tent. If he'd snuck into the tomb just after Leila screamed, it would have been about an hour ago, what with all our stumbling around down here trying to find the staircase.

I could see Volsky uncovering the chamber in that amount of time, if he worked hard and fast.

We followed the sound, tiptoeing down the passageway, stopping every few feet to listen again. We turned left, then right, then right again, and finally we found the set of stairs leading down to the burial chamber.

There was no need to listen anymore. We knew the way from here. We ran down the stairs and picked our way through the rubble that had hidden the chamber before Volsky moved it.

I don't know what I expected to see when we entered the chamber—Volsky had to have heard us coming the minute we hit the staircase, and gave up trying to be quiet—but what we *didn't* see was a total shock.

Not only had Volsky vanished—so had the Golden Mummy!

13.
A Woman of Hidden Talents

There was no mummy inside the stone sarcophagus. Maybe there never had been. There was no treasure in the room either.

Everyone looked disappointed. "Where's the famous treasure?" Tommy wondered.

"Dr. Volsky must have been really upset when he realized there wasn't any loot to steal," Joe said.

"He must have been even more surprised when there wasn't any mummy," I said.

"Maybe there was one," Sam said. "Maybe he lifted the mummy on his shoulders and ran away with it, farther into the tomb."

"Or maybe it chased him!" Ahmed said.

"Aw, man," Theo moaned, "we missed the shot

again! Nels, you didn't bother to turn on that camera when we ran in here, did you?"

"Me? Why was that *my* job?" Nels shot back. "We were chasing Volsky. No one thought of it—not me, not Jurgen, and not you, either."

I thought the three of them might start punching each other, they looked so frustrated. Finally, Nels went back out into the passageway, brought the camera inside, and started taping the scene.

Tommy was pounding the stone walls with his fists. That had to hurt, but he didn't seem to care.

Meanwhile, Samantha was examining the stone sarcophagus itself. She reached her hand inside it and drew out a scroll.

"It is an ancient papyrus!" Ahmed gasped in wonder. "Be careful; it may crumble before you can read it!"

Sam unrolled it, little by little. She stared at the hieroglyphics and shook her head. "What does it mean?" she asked aloud.

Leila and Ahmed were staring at it over her shoulder. "Don't look at me," said Ahmed with a shrug. "I am only the Happy Hippie. You are the one who went to university, miss."

Leila shook her head. "I can't read it either," she said.

Something about the look on her face, though, told me she might have understood at least some of the writing—enough to frighten and disturb her.

I wondered if anyone else had seen that momentary flicker in her eyes. I hoped not.

Jurgen held the light high overhead, while Nels taped the papyrus, zooming in close.

Tommy was still steaming. Now he stopped punching the wall and turned his rage on Samantha instead. "You are so stupid! You brought us all this way, and for what? For nothing!"

"ME? *I'm* stupid?" Samantha shot back. "Maybe you're right—I was stupid to fall for a brainless wonder like you!"

"Ha! You should talk!"

"What good are you, anyway? Those big muscles are totally useless, Tommy. And you know where the biggest muscle of all is?" She tapped him on his forehead—hard. "THERE!"

The video crew immediately started taping the big fight between the leader of the expedition and her boyfriend. Joe tried to get between Tommy and Samantha, and Ahmed tried to restrain Tommy.

While everyone else was distracted, I took Leila by the hand and led her outside the burial chamber.

"What is it?" she asked.

"You understood that scroll," I said. "You know what it says, don't you?"

"I . . ."

"Tell me the truth, Leila! It's our only hope!"

She took a deep breath. "All right," she said. "I will tell you. You are not arrogant like Samantha and Tommy. I believe I can trust you."

She glanced back inside the chamber, where the fight was starting to calm down. "The scroll said, 'You who have come to desecrate my tomb and steal what is mine—you will die before the next full moon. You shall never possess my greatest treasure, for it lives with me and my beloved. We lie nearby, in eternal peace, where no eyes can see.'"

"The full moon . . . that's tomorrow night, isn't it?"

Leila nodded. "We have only one day left to live, it says."

"You don't believe that, do you?"

"I believe that if we do not leave this place tomorrow, we will all die here."

I didn't disagree with her. The danger did seem to be mounting, with the killer—who was looking more and more like Volsky—on the loose.

"We've got to tell Joe," I said.

"Why?" Leila looked alarmed.

"It's okay; he's my brother. He's on our side, take my word for it."

"But he will tell Samantha! He loves her, can you not see it?"

"He won't if I tell him not to," I assured her. "We've got to let him in on the secret. Together, the three of us can think of something."

We reentered the burial chamber just as the group was plotting its next move.

"Now, what about Volsky?" Samantha asked. "We've got to find him before he gets away with—"

"With what?" interrupted Leila. "What exactly could he have taken with him? Do you think there was treasure in this chamber? If there had been, there would have been a lot of it."

"With the mummy itself, maybe?" Ahmed suggested.

"Maybe," Theo said, frowning. "Anyway, we've got to find him, and fast. He could have read that scroll easily—and maybe it leads to the treasure, if there is one."

"I agree," I said. "We'll split up and start searching. Same method—tear off some strips of cloth from your shirts and robes to mark which way you went. We'll all meet up back here in an hour—hopefully, with Volsky in tow."

We broke into teams. I made sure that our team

consisted of me, Leila, and Joe. Tommy, Nels, and Jurgen made up a second team. Samantha, Ahmed, and Theo made up the third.

Theo and Nels carried the two cameras, to record their teams' progress. Even with everyone's life on the line, it seemed, the taping still had to go on.

Once the other two teams had gone off in search of Volsky, I told Joe what the inscription on the scroll said.

He whistled softly. "So this isn't the real burial chamber at all!" he said.

"At least we know the real one's nearby," I said. "The other two teams will be searching all over the place. We'll search close to this spot. That gives us an advantage, right?"

"But without the map, I don't know how we're ever going to find it," Joe said. "With all these passage-ways, it could take days—weeks, even. And mean-while, Volsky's got the map. He can get away with as much treasure as he can carry, and be gone before we find anything!"

"You think one of us should guard the camels, to make sure he can't make a run for it?" I asked.

Joe looked at Leila, then shook his head. "It would have to be one of us," he said to me. "She wouldn't be able to overpower him."

"Who says I couldn't?" Leila said, insulted.

"Besides," I added, "we're not even sure Volsky knows where the real burial chamber is. He probably didn't find that papyrus scroll, or he would have taken it with him."

"He has the map," Joe pointed out. "Corson had found the real chamber, remember, because he said it contained huge amounts of treasure. So the map is everything."

"But who says Volsky's the one who has it?" I argued.

"Duh, isn't it obvious?"

"Not really. The guy who stole it from Sam, we'd decided, worked for Mounir, so he probably stole it for him—except whoever killed him took it before it could be handed over. We can't assume that was Volsky."

"If it wasn't, then why did he sneak into the burial chamber by himself?" Joe asked.

"Maybe he just wanted to get there first," I said. "That guiding fire changed things, remember. It showed us all where the mummy was—or at least, that's what we all thought till now. Remember, if Volsky had the map, he would have known where the real burial chamber was. But he still had to see what was in the chamber we'd found. The mystery must have been irresistible."

"Well, the fact is, without the map, we're still flying blind," Joe said with a sigh.

"No," Leila said, looking from me to Joe and back at me again. "We are not lost."

"Huh?"

"I have the map," she said.

I was floored. "*You* stole Sam's map?" I said. "You mean, you—"

"No, it is not like you think," she told us. "I did not take it from her tent. And I did not kill the man who took it."

"Then how . . ."

"I was afraid it would be stolen, and lost to those of us who want to preserve it for the people of Egypt—so I snuck into Samantha's tent . . . and I copied it."

Her lips curled into a sly smile as she held up her hennaed hands. "Here is the map that will lead us to the mummy's treasure, and the source of the curse we have all been under."

I stared in amazement at the miniature map Leila had drawn on her hands and arms, and wondered at how brave and clever she was.

If she ever got tired of archaeology, I had a feeling there was a job ready for her at ATAC.

JOE

14.
Secrets of the Tomb

The Tomb of the Golden Mummy was built as a maze. That much was obvious. If you've ever been in one of those hedge mazes they have in corn-fields, you'll know what it felt like.

But this maze was dark and creepy, and Dr. Volsky was somewhere in the darkness, lurking, lying in wait with whatever weapon he happened to have on him.

Luckily, while the other two teams were searching blind, we had Leila's map. I had to hand it to her, she'd been smarter than any of us, copying it onto her hands that way.

She led us now, seemingly in circles, but the scraps of clothing we left as markers did not reappear, so I guessed we had to be covering new ground.

For a while we heard the sounds of the other groups. But after descending another staircase and edging through a narrow passageway, we found ourselves in a whole new section of the tomb. Here there was only silence—until we heard a scampering noise up ahead in the darkness.

Frank shone his flashlight that way, but whatever it was dodged behind a corner of the stone wall. We followed, carefully. None of us was armed, after all.

The skittering sound led us onward. "It is taking us in the right direction," Leila said, examining the map on her hands.

We rounded another corner and were greeted by a loud screeching noise. A huge shadow rose up over us—a shadow that wasn't quite human.

Frank aimed his flashlight at the source of the shadow: a large, angry-looking monkey! What it was doing in here, and how it managed to feed itself (on spiders, maybe?) was a mystery.

The monkey scampered away from us, disappearing down a side passageway to the left. "Should we follow it?" I asked.

Leila checked her hands, then nodded. We followed the monkey's retreat, rounding a sharp corner—and found ourselves at one end of a long, high-ceilinged passageway. Halfway to the other end of the passage stood Dr. Volsky!

"Volsky!" Frank yelled. "Stop where you are!"

Volsky stumbled backward, surprised by our sudden appearance and blinded by the light of Frank's flashlight shining in his eyes. "You! How did you find me?"

"Never mind that. Hand over the map!" I ordered.

"Map? I have no map!" He started slowly backing away from us. We didn't have to chase him, though—there was nothing but a big, blank wall behind him.

"Sure you do," I said. "Corson's map. You killed the camel driver to get it. Now hand it over."

"I killed no one," he insisted, "and I have no map."

"Then how did you find this place?" Frank asked.

"The same way you did—our monkey friend."

"Well, if you didn't kill anyone," I asked, "who did?"

Volsky kept backing away until he bumped up against the wall at the far end of the passage. His hand reached out and touched a stone on the wall.

Not just any stone, though—this one was carved with an ankh, one of the most common Egyptian hieroglyphs.

The moment Volsky touched the stone, it slid right into the wall. The next thing we knew, the wall slid open in the middle!

Volsky staggered toward us. A loud rumbling came from behind the wall that was sliding open.

Then I saw what was causing it: a huge, black stone ball was rolling right down the passage, headed straight for Volsky—and us.

Volsky screamed and ran toward us, but not fast enough. The stone ball caught up with him and rolled right over him, crushing him!

We didn't stop to think—there was no time for that. We made it to the end of the passageway and leaped out of the way, just as the stone ball hit the wall behind us, smashing into a thousand pieces.

"Everyone all right?" Frank asked when the smoke and dust cleared.

"I'm fine," Leila said.

"Me too," I said. "But I think Volsky might not be."

We made our way past the jagged pieces of the stone ball, to where Volsky lay in the passageway.

He was obviously dead—a victim of the Golden Mummy's curse?

Beyond his body, the entrance to the Golden Mummy's real burial chamber was wide open before us, lit by torches. We walked up to the door and peeked inside.

In the center of the room were two golden sarcophagi—the Golden Mummy and his beloved, I guessed. The coffins were surrounded by piles of priceless objects, all made of gold and jewels.

We'd found the mummy's treasure!

"Aha, there you are!" came a man's voice from behind us.

We wheeled around and were blinded by a light much brighter than a flashlight's.

"Thank you so much for finding the treasure for me."

The light went out, and we saw that it was Theo, holding his camera as usual. He put it down now and held up something else that he drew from his pocket.

A gun!

Cocking it and leveling it at us, he said, "It's too bad you won't live to enjoy it."

15.
The Riddle Solved

"Theo!" Joe said. "Well, I have to say, you had me fooled. I wouldn't have pegged you for a stone killer."

"I was an actor before I became a director," Theo said, smiling at the compliment.

"So you killed the camel driver to get the map?" I asked.

He nodded his head. "Correct. Too bad, it was a complete waste of effort—I didn't need to kill him, as it turned out. You see, I hadn't planned on you, Miss Leila, sneaking into Samantha's tent and copying the map onto your hands.

"My videotape would have told me everything I needed to know—but by the time I figured that

148

out, I'd already killed both the driver and Mounir."

Leila looked at her temporary tattoos now, as if they were some useless thing, or worse. "I did not know about the camera," she said, "or I would have hidden the map better."

"It wouldn't have mattered," Theo said. "I would have taken care to follow your passage through the tomb the minute you broke away from the rest of the group. There is no way you could have kept me in the dark."

"What makes you think you won't get zapped by the mummy's curse?" I asked. "After all, look what happened to Dr. Volsky."

Theo snickered. "Do you think I believe in that nonsense? I am a self-made man, my boy. I learned how to lie and steal from my own father, and my grandfather, too."

"I suppose Jurgen and Nels are in on the whole thing," Joe said.

Theo smiled. "My cousins. We're a very talented family of thieves and con men, not to mention artists."

"And murderers," Joe added. "Don't forget that."

"Now, now. I always try to avoid killing people. So messy."

"What about Roger Corson?" I asked.

Theo's smile vanished. "Oh. Him. Well, it wasn't planned that way, I assure you. It just made me furious that he'd given the map to that moronic girlfriend of his. So when I heard that he'd done that, I couldn't help killing him."

"So that was you in the mummy suit," I said.

"Just so. And on the boat, also. Costumes are something I know well from my acting days. But I meant what I said—I don't enjoy killing. I try to avoid it."

Theo sighed. "Killing you three will make things even worse. I'm so sorry—not that that's going to stop me. After all," he added, looking past us into the chamber, where the incredible pile of gold and jewels twinkled in the light of the wall torches, "that's quite a haul in there. It would be a shame to let someone else have it."

"Like the Egyptian people?" Leila said, her voice full of outrage. "It's theirs! It belongs to them, and you have no right to take it."

Theo sighed sadly. "I have to agree with you, Miss Leila," he said. "But you see, I'm just a very bad man. I've already tried to get rid of you all once—Miss Leila with the snake, and you boys with the scorpions."

"What's the matter," Joe said, sneering, "you don't like getting too close to your victims?"

Theo looked unbearably sad. "So true. You know, you're making me really hate myself for what I'm about to do."

"Then don't do it!" I shouted. "You don't have to. If you turn yourself in . . ."

"Then what? I'll get life in prison? Joy." Theo held up the gun and pointed it right at Joe. "No, I don't think I'll do that."

Just then, Nels and Jurgen showed up, their pistols aimed at the backs of Ahmed, Tommy, and Samantha, who all held their hands high in the air.

"Ah, now our party is complete!" Theo said happily. "Good. Now you will please all march down the corridor, that way."

He pointed away from the treasure chamber and to the left. "Yes, into that long, narrow chamber. That's it. . . ."

We did as he said. Theo, Jurgen, and Nels stood in the doorway—the only entrance to the chamber— while the rest of us waited to die.

"There," said Theo. "Ah, what a wonderful map Roger Corson made. So instructive." He reached up and to his right, where another stone etched with an ankh protruded from the wall. "And now, I'm afraid it's time to say good-bye."

He pushed on the stone, and it slid into the wall. There was a heavy, grinding noise, and suddenly, the back wall started moving forward, pushing us toward the entrance where Theo and his gang stood.

A second later, the half of the floor between us and the entrance gave way, revealing a twenty-foot-long, ten-foot-deep pit, filled with hissing, poisonous snakes.

We couldn't leap across the pit to the entrance, and the back wall kept inching forward bit by bit. Soon we would be forced to jump right into the snake pit!

"Come on, boys," Theo told Nels and Jurgen, and the three of them went off to gather up the mummy's treasure.

"Now what?" Joe asked me as we watched their retreating figures disappear around the corner of the passageway.

There was no time to think, so I just said what came into my head. "There's only one way out of here," I said. "And that's down into the snake pit and out the other side."

"Are you kidding me?" Joe said. "No possible way!"

"We're done for!" Tommy said. He turned to Samantha, furious. "Now look at the mess you've gotten us into!"

"Me?" Sam shot back, jumping into the argument and forgetting completely about the fact that our lives were about to be snuffed out. "This is all your fault! You were the one who interviewed the video crew and recommended them!"

"Well, they were cool guys!" Tommy said. "How was I supposed to know they were crooked?"

"Just be quiet, the two of you!" Leila cried out, in a voice that made them stop at once.

"If you'll permit me," Ahmed spoke up in the silence. "I think I may be able to help us get out of here."

"You?" Tommy said with a snicker. "What are you gonna do, cook up something for the snakes?"

Ahmed smiled a wily smile. "In a way, yes," he said. "May I?"

The back wall was getting closer—it was only about six feet from the edge of the pit now, with all of us scrunched together in the small space between the wall and the snake pit.

"Go ahead," Sam said.

"Thank you, madam," Ahmed said. He reached into his sleeve and pulled out what looked like a flute.

"Oh, are you kidding me?" Tommy said, flailing his arms in frustration. "You're gonna play music now?"

"Shhhh!" Leila said, and Tommy did.

Ahmed started playing a sultry tune. Immediately, the slithering pile of snakes came to a halt. The snakes lifted their heads and swayed to the music, as if hypnotized by the melody.

"I don't believe this!" Tommy said. "The guy's a snake charmer, too!"

Not only was he a snake charmer, he was a very good one. Quickly, before the snakes came to their senses, we lowered ourselves into the pit and tiptoed our way across, careful not to touch any of the swaying serpents along the way. It was tricky lowering Ahmed while he kept playing his flute, but we managed it somehow.

At the far end, I put Leila on my shoulders and helped her out. We all raised Ahmed up together so he could keep up the tune. He didn't stop playing for a second. It was pretty impressive, I have to admit.

"Tommy," I said, "now it's your turn to hoist the rest of us—put all that brute strength to some good use for a change."

He gave me a snarl, but did as I told him, hoisting us out one after the other as if we were made of feathers.

Finally, we all pulled together to yank him up. He made it over the edge just as the back wall clanged into its final position at the other edge of the snake pit.

We'd have all been dead by then, if it hadn't been for the Happy Hippie and his fantastic flute.

And to think, he'd only come along at the last minute, and only because he played a trick on Dr. Mounir's chosen cook!

We all rushed down the passage to the treasure chamber. Theo, Nels, and Jurgen were caught completely by surprise. They had all put their guns back in their belts, and their arms were piled high with treasure—so high that their view of us was blocked until we were almost on top of them.

Between Joe's kung fu moves and Tommy's knockout punches, we got the upper hand quickly. But the biggest surprise was Ahmed, who whirled into action and showed some martial arts moves that Joe and I had never seen before.

"Whoa!" I said, my jaw dropping. "Ahmed, you are a man of many talents."

"I'll say!" Joe agreed. "Where'd you learn to fight like that?"

Ahmed smiled and gave us a little salute as he finished hog-tying the last of the three vicious videographers. "Lieutenant Ahmed Hussein, of the Egyptian Special Police, at your service," he said, producing an official badge from his pocket.

"Egyptian Special Police?" Sam repeated. "You mean—"

"Yes, Miss Samantha," said the Happy Hippie. "I was assigned by my government to come along on your expedition and protect your life—and the lives of these two young men," he added, putting an arm on Joe's and my shoulders.

"Our lives?" I said. "Who in the Egyptian government thought we needed protection?"

"Captain Ali," Ahmed said. "He sends his apologies. He did not mean to insult your talents—but he just wanted to make sure that the sons of Fenton Hardy came to no harm."

"I can't believe it," Joe said. I could see he felt a little insulted. "What made them think we couldn't handle the job alone?"

Ahmed smiled. "Just after you left for Ras Khalifa," he said, "Captain Ali received word from Interpol of a plot by an international criminal gang to steal the Golden Mummy's treasure."

"So all that Happy Hippie stuff . . ." Tommy said, slowly letting it sink into his thick skull.

"I am sorry to have deceived everyone," Ahmed said, giving a little bow with his hands held together. "But I hope my cooking was satisfactory."

"It was better than that," Sam assured him.

"It sure was," Joe said. "And you know what my favorite dish was? Hard-boiled crooks, well done."

"Yeah," I agreed, slapping Lieutenant Ahmed on the back, "*very* well done!"

16.
Echoes of Egypt

Bayport's annual fair was in full swing the day after Frank and I got back from Egypt. They do it out at Gormley Park, which used to be a really big farm. For one weekend a year, it turns into a full-scale carnival, with rides, 4-H stuff like pig-judging contests, and all kinds of live performances.

Frank and I were dog tired and jet-lagged, so we might have slept in and missed all the fun if Chet and Iola hadn't stopped by and rung the doorbell.

"Come on!" Chet demanded, barging into our room and yanking the pillows out from under our heads. "I can smell the fried dough all the way across town!"

Chet, to put it bluntly, eats too much every day of his life. But the weekend of the Bayport Fair, he throws all restraint to the wind and goes totally hog-wild. It's a riot, just watching him as he packs it away—all kinds of junk food, from burgers and franks to . . . well, to fried dough.

Yuck.

Iola said, "I'll be downstairs—hurry up!" and left us to get dressed.

Half an hour later we all hit the fairgrounds. The first thing that struck me as weird was the gigantic pyramid. There it stood, smack in the middle of the field.

"What in the—?" Frank said, stopping in his tracks when he saw it.

"Oh, yeah," Iola said, grinning. "It's an Egyptian theme this year. Check out the big slide over there."

She pointed to a slide that looked like a sphinx with a long, steel tongue, down which kids were riding in a steady stream.

"Can you believe this?" I asked Frank.

"No way," he said.

"They're saying Samantha Chilton's new reality show is going to be awesome!" Iola said. "It's all the rage. Are you guys seriously starring in it? 'Cause that's what I heard. How on earth did you get on the show? Oh wait, don't tell me—just Hardy luck. Always in the right place at the right time."

Uh . . . sure.

"I don't know about 'starring,'" Frank said modestly.

"That is so cool!" Iola said, clapping her hands. "Can I, like, have your autographs?"

I wasn't sure how we'd explain the whole *Beautiful People* thing—but I figured we'd cross that bridge when we got to it. I smiled, took out a pencil, and scribbled my name on the napkin Iola had spread on Frank's back.

"Omigosh, I know them!" Chet said, mimicking her.

Just then, this really annoying mime came up to us. He was painted all in gold, he had King Tut's famous multicolored hat on, and he started doing that funky Egyptian head movement from side to side.

"Hey," I said, "thanks, but could you go do your thing for somebody else?"

He ignored me, doing the head and neck thing right in Frank's and my face, backing us up until we were quite a ways from Chet and Iola.

"Excuse me," Frank said to the guy, "but we

haven't seen our friends in a long time, and we'd like to hang with them, okay? Thanks for understanding."

But the guy didn't seem to understand at all. He kept it up, and now, reaching into his golden skirt thingy, he drew out a golden DVD and handed it to me.

"What?" I asked. "Are you selling this or something?"

"We don't want to buy anything," Frank said, taking the DVD from me and handing it back to the mime. "Please. Could you just leave us alone?"

But the mime kept on doing his thing, right in our faces. Talk about annoying!

"Take a hike, pal," I said, stepping up close to golden boy.

He didn't budge.

"Frank?"

Frank took hold of one elbow, I took the other, and we lifted "King Tut" off the ground, escorting him to a better location, about fifty feet away.

"Take a hint next time," I told him, wiping the gold paint off my hands as Frank and I turned to go back to where our friends were waiting.

"Hey!" the mime suddenly said. "Do you want your next case, or don't you?"

Duh!

"Sure thing," I said, taking the jewel case from him. "We'll take it—as long as it doesn't come with a mummy's curse attached!"

Exciting fiction from three-time Newbery Honor author Gary Paulsen

Newbery Honor Book

Newbery Honor Book

Aladdin Paperbacks and Simon Pulse
Simon & Schuster Children's Publishing
www.SimonSays.com

agine a world where families are allowed only two children.

egal third children—shadow children—must live in hiding,

for if they are discovered, there is only one punishment:

Death.

Read the Shadow Children series by

MARGARET PETERSON HADDIX

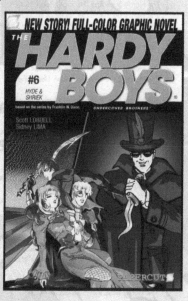

CLUE IN TO THE CLASSIC MYSTERIES OF THE HARDY BOYS®
FROM GROSSET & DUNLAP

$7.99 ($10.99 CAN) each

AVAILABLE AT YOUR LOCAL BOOKSTORE OR LIBRARY

Grosset & Dunlap • A division of Penguin Young Readers Group
A member of Penguin Group (USA), Inc. • A Pearson Company
www.penguin.com/youngreaders

THE HARDY BOYS is a trademark of Simon & Schuster, Inc., registered in the United States Patent and Trademark Office.